13 Tennessee Ghosts

and Jeffrey

With Love And Gratitude For My Children

Kitti, Ben, And Dilcy

Who Have Put Up With A Lot

From Me — And Jeffrey

13 Tennessee Ghosts
and Jeffrey

COMMEMORATIVE EDITION

Kathryn Tucker Windham

With a New Afterword by
Dilcy Windham Hilley and Ben Windham

THE UNIVERSITY OF ALABAMA PRESS
Tuscaloosa

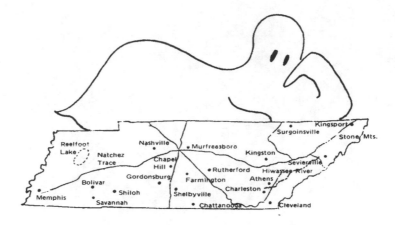

The University of Alabama Press
Tuscaloosa, Alabama 35487-0380
uapress.ua.edu

Hardcover edition published 2016.
Paperback edition published 2021.
eBook edition published 2016.

Typeface: Times New Roman

Photographs by Kathryn Tucker Windham (unless otherwise indicated)
Illustrated by Lecia Brogdon
Cover design: Karl Scott

Paperback ISBN: 978-0-8173-6035-1

A previous edition of this book has been cataloged by the Library of Congress.
ISBN: 978-0-8173-1901-4 (cloth)
E-ISBN: 978-0-8173-8947-5

Contents

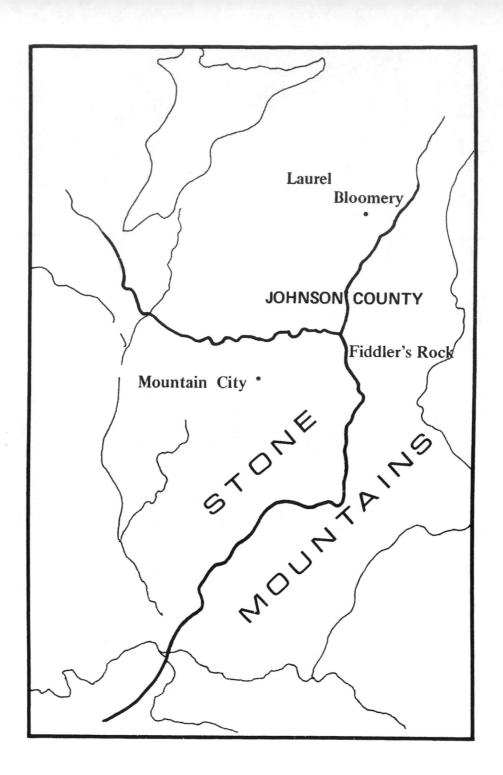

The Snake Charmer

Sometimes on summer nights, when moonlight softens the rough profiles of Stone Mountains, snatches of fiddle music drift from Fiddler's Rock. The tunes change, blend, swell, fade, and swell again as though a distant fiddler were warming up for a performance.

Not everyone hears the music. And some mountaineers, especially the younger ones, say it is not music at all but the sound of wind rushing down from high rocks and swishing through the trees and losing itself in the twisting coves and hollows. Others say it is only the music from record players or radios bouncing against the cliffs and echoing into the valleys.

But other mountain dwellers hear the tunes plainly, recognize the distinctive style of the fiddler.

"Listen," they say. "Listen. Old Martin is playing tonight. What's that? 'Cripple Creek'! Hear it? Just as plain. That's old Martin, all right. Up there charming his snakes. Bet that old flat rock is thick with rattlers now, crawling out of their dens to hear Martin play his fiddle. Old Martin. The snake charmer. Just listen...."

It has been better than a hundred years—closer maybe to a century and a quarter—since Martin lived up in Johnson County, Tennessee. Some folks say he was born near Trace, and others claim his family lived not far from Elk Mills.

Wherever it was that Martin was born, he grew up in those rugged east Tennessee mountains. He hunted and he fished and he trapped, when he wasn't helping his daddy cut logs. Long before most boys could even open a jack knife, Martin was whittling little wooden figures of animals—squirrels and rabbits and bears and such. His grandfather taught him how to see a creature in a piece of wood.

His grandfather taught Martin how to play the fiddle, too. He taught him to play the old tunes brought over from England, the staid hymns, the dancing play-party rhythms, and the wailing laments for times long past.

With his grandfather's help, Martin made his first fiddle, whittling it out of seasoned wood and carving decorations on it to suit his fancy.

By the time he was half grown, Martin had the name of being the best fiddler in Johnson County. He played for weddings, and he played for funerals. He played for barn raisings, and he played for church sociables. He played for dances, and he played for idlers sitting around the store down at the crossroads. He could play any tune anybody called for, and he made up a hundred or more tunes of his own.

"Tunes are just singing around in my head. I can hear them as plain as anything," Martin told folks who asked where he got his new melodies.

Neighbors used to say that if a restless, fretful baby was brought within earshot of Martin's fiddling, the baby would quit crying and drop off to sleep as peaceful as you please. It was like magic.

There was even some belief that Martin's music had curative powers, that it could make sick people well. Martin himself never made any such claims, though he was perfectly willing to go wherever he was asked to play for someone who was ailing.

"If my music helps them get well, that's fine. If it doesn't, at least maybe I've given them a little joyful time." Joyful times were important to Martin.

Up around Laurel Bloomery, they used to say that Martin had the only singing mule in the mountains. They said Martin would be playing his fiddle while he rode his mule, riding bareback the way he always did, and every now and then the mule would bray in time to the music. Some folks even said the mule's bray was in harmony with the fiddle and that anybody who halfway listened could recognize the song the mule brayed. That could have been true. Maybe.

When Martin played for dances, they say listeners forgot their rheumatism and their stiff joints and were out on the floor stomping up a dust before Martin had played six measures of "Sourwood Mountain." "Even the preachers can't help dancing when Martin plays," they used to say.

People at Pandora, some of them, swore that Martin hunted with his fiddle. He used to go into the woods without a gun or any kind of weapon, just take his fiddle, and in a little while he'd come out with his hunting sack full of squirrels. All his pockets would be full, too. And not a one of those squirrels ever had a mark on them. Not everybody believed that tale.

But just about everybody who heard him play believed that Martin was the finest fiddler in east Tennessee. Maybe he was the finest fiddler in the whole state: middle Tennessee wasn't much known for fiddling, and not many Johnson Countians had ever been as far away as west Tennessee so they couldn't accurately judge. But in east Tennessee, where music was appreciated and respected, even the oldest fiddlers agreed that Martin handled the bow better than any music-maker they'd ever heard.

Such praise didn't make Martin proud or strutified. "I can't paint pictures, and I ain't never made much success at farming, and I didn't do good in school, and I can't sing—not even as good as my mule can—and I can't make speeches. But the Good Lord talented me with fiddling. So that's how I want to be remembered: long after I'm dead and gone, I want folks to recollect how I played my fiddle."

Well, one afternoon Martin was sitting on the edge of the store porch playing his fiddle, entertaining the idlers, when Absalom Stanley rode up and tied his mule to a post by the steps.

Soon as Martin finished playing the piece he had started, Absalom asked, "Martin, reckon you can charm snakes with your music?"

Martin thought a minute, and then he said he never had once considered doing such a thing, and he didn't know if he wanted to try, and he wondered why Absalom would ask such a question.

"It's my boy, Polk. He wants to know," Absalom said. "He brought his geography book home from school, and that book tells about men somewhere—Indy, I think it is—who play little horns and charm snakes. Even make them dance. Soon as my boy, Polk, read that, he said, 'I bet Martin can charm snakes with his fiddle.' Can you?"

Martin didn't answer right away. Nobody had ever asked him such a question before. He sat there on the store porch studying about it. He laid his fiddle across his knees and picked the strings with his thumb and forefinger while he

Over a century ago the best fiddler in Johnson County, Tennessee, used to charm snakes with his music in the rugged east Tennessee mountains.

thought. He picked those strings a pretty good while, not making any kind of a tune, before he said, "Charming snakes ain't a easy thing to do. At least I don't figure it is. Never heard of anybody around here doing it. But maybe I can. Bring Polk's book tomorrow afternoon and let me read about it. Then I'll see what I think."

Then Martin took his fiddle and got on his mule and headed home.

News about Martin's upcoming decision spread fast, and the next afternoon there was a sizable crowd gathered on the store porch. Martin entertained them with music until Absalom got there with Polk's geography book.

Absalom handed the book to Martin, and Martin, though he wasn't the best reader in the county, read aloud the short paragraph about the Indian snake charmer.

The men were quiet as a cistern while Martin read, but as soon as he stopped, one of them asked, "You reckon that's really so? Reckon them men do charm snakes with their playing?"

"Must be so," Martin replied. "They got a picture here of a little old man squatting down on his haunches and playing a horn, and a funny looking snake is reared up right in front of him, looking him in the eye. It must be so."

He passed the book around for them all to see.

"Don't reckon that cloth wrapped around the fellow's head has anything to do with his power over the snakes, do you?" one of the men looking at the sketch asked. "Don't know as we could get Martin's head wrapped up like that!"

"It ain't the head-wrapping that bothers me," Martin replied. "I just wish I could hear a sample of the tune the man is playing. I don't know whether it takes a dancing tune or a doleful melody to charm a snake."

"You're gonna do it, then?" Absalom asked.

"I'm gonna try," Martin replied. "If snakes in Indy can

12

be charmed, so can snakes in Tennessee. Snakes is snakes."

"When you aiming to do it?"

"Tomorrow, I reckon. Too late today, not enough daylight left. I'll set out in the morning, not too early, for that flat ledge up on the mountain. By the time I get there, the sun will be pretty high, and the snakes'll be coming out of their dens to stretch out on the rock ledge and warm themselves. I'll sort of ease in there, me and my fiddle, and see how they like my music."

One or two of the older men in the crowd cautioned Martin about fooling around with rattlesnakes, but Martin had made up his mind.

So the next morning Martin, astride his mule, set out with his fiddle for Stone Mountains. He guided the mule up the steep path as far as the footing was safe. Then he tethered the animal to a stout sapling and continued to climb afoot.

Martin climbed over rough boulders and skirted deep crevices, brushing against clumps of rhododendron and laurel, until he reached the flat ledge where he intended to stage his experiment. Then he settled himself on a rock, a big one shaped like a footstool, near the center of the ledge and began to play.

He started off slowly, playing a gentle melody. Then he picked up the tempo, and he played a little louder, sort of coaxing the snakes out of their hiding places.

Out of the corner of his eye, Martin saw a rattler ease out of a rock pile and glide toward him. Martin played a little louder and a little faster. The snake—he was monstrous big— slid up closer and then stretched out full length on the gray rock.

Martin kept playing. He was careful not to pat his foot—and the naturalness of beating a rhythm with his foot was hard to control—fearing the movement might cause a snake to strike. Only his fingers on the strings and his hand

13

wielding the bow moved. And his eyes: they moved almost constantly as Martin watched the arrival of other snakes who came to share the concert.

Pretty soon there were almost a dozen rattlers out on the ledge. They weren't exactly charmed, Martin decided, but his music had lured them out of their dens, and they were all still and quiet.

Martin knew, having grown up in the wilds, that snakes have no ears, so it stood to reason they couldn't hear the tunes he was playing. They were attracted, he decided, not by the beauty of his music but by the vibrations of the sound waves.

After awhile, Martin got tired: even the world's finest fiddler can't keep playing forever. He was uneasy, too, not knowing what the snakes would do if he quit playing. He gradually slowed the pace and the volume of his music until it trailed off into nothingness. Then he eased his fiddle and his bow across his knees and sat there as still as the stone he had chosen for his stage.

Maybe it was half an hour, maybe longer, before the snakes began to crawl away, heading back to wherever it was they had come from. Martin was muchly relieved: he didn't know what he would have done if they had decided to stay.

But they did leave, all except one. That one snake and Martin looked at each other for a long time. Finally Martin decided the snake was asleep (it's hard to be sure: a snake has no eyelids to close). Martin took a stout stick with a small fork on the end, and he quickly pinned the snake to the ledge. Then he crushed the writhing reptile's head with the heel of his boot.

He dropped the dead snake into his hunting bag, and he climbed down the mountain to where his mule was waiting.

As soon as he got in sight of the store, Martin could tell there was a big crowd waiting for him.

14

"Did you charm them snakes?" somebody hollered.

"Sure did!" Martin called back.

Martin sat on the porch and munched cheese and crackers (he hadn't realized how hungry he was) while he told his listeners everything that had happened. Parts of his story he repeated half a dozen times. Then he showed them the snake he had brought back.

"He's not so big—most of them were a lot bigger," Martin said half apologetically.

The men stretched the snake out on the floor, and the storekeeper measured it: five feet, eight and one-quarter inches, counting the rattles.

Martin took the snake home with him, skinned it, and tacked the skin up on the side of the smokehouse to dry. He drapped the brown rattles down into his fiddle as a sort of a good luck charm.

At first Martin thought one effort, and a rather successful one, to charm rattlesnakes would be enough, but it didn't satisfy the populace of Johnson County (seems that as word about the snake-charming spread, more and more people got interested in it), and it didn't fully satisfy Martin either.

So he went back again. Again he played for the snakes, and again they responded to his music. And again Martin brought back a big snake, quite dead, to show off at the store.

It finally got to where Martin was going up to the ledge three or four times a week to play for the snakes. He had a feeling sometimes that they were waiting for him, that they missed him when he didn't come.

A story got started around the region (whether Martin himself told it or not is uncertain) that the snakes—at least some of them—got to where they would shake their rattles in time to Martin's music.

Anyhow, Martin kept giving those concerts for a long

One night Martin must have dropped his bow, reached down to retrieve it, and been bitten. The snakes chewed him up something awful.

time. His whole smokehouse was covered with the drying skins of trophies he brought home.

Then Martin got to wondering if the rattlers would come out to hear him play at night. He wondered about it for a week or two, and since there wasn't anybody to ask, he determined to find out for himself.

One moonlight night, a warm night in early September, Martin followed the familiar trail up Stone Mountains to

16

where the jutting ledge of rock formed his strange concert hall.

It was Martin's last trip up that mountain.

About daylight the next morning, a rider passing along the valley road heard a mule braying in a peculiar way. He found Martin's mule tethered on the slope of the mountain where Martin always left him.

A search party found Martin's body lying on the trail, about halfway down the mountain. Fang marks, more than two dozen of them, pocked his swollen hands and face. His fiddle was lying beside him, but his bow was missing.

While some of the men took Martin's body home, a few others continued the climb up the mountain to look around the ledge. These searchers found Martin's missing bow lying beside the round rock where Martin sat during his concerts.

Nobody is fully certain what happened. It appears that Martin got careless, just for an instant. He must have dropped his bow, reached down in the shadows to pick it up (he knew better—he momentarily forgot the deadliness of his audience), and been bitten by a rattler. Other reptiles joined in the attack, thrusting their fangs into the hands that had played for them, had tried to charm them.

They still talk about Martin up there in east Tennessee. His performances gave the name to the ledge high up on Stone Mountains where he played to the snakes: Fiddler's Rock, natives call it.

And on summer nights when fiddle tunes drift softly from the isolated heights of Fiddler's Rock, folks who hear the music recall Martin and his music.

"Listen," they say. "Listen. It's Martin playing his fiddle to charm the snakes. I reckon he'll be playing up there forever."

17

During the Great Flood of 1867 the southbound train crossed the Hiwassee River and eased toward the Charleston depot. It wrecked near this building.

The Rosary

Dr. J. Lake McClary, M.D., had worked all day moving books, medical instruments, and furniture into his new office in Charleston, and he was very tired. He did not welcome the intrusion of the stranger who stopped in the doorway to gaze around the office.

"Looks like you're about to get moved in, Dr. McClary," the stranger said. "I'm Hornsby." He extended his hand.

Dr. McClary shifted his armload of books and shook hands with his visitor. "Yes, I'm making progress," he replied. He was in no mood for interruptions of any kind, but he did not wish to appear rude.

"Don't look like you've got a skeleton in your office," the visitor observed. "The old doc—the one who was here before you came—set a real store by the skeleton he had. You ain't got one?"

"No. No skeleton."

Dr. McClary knew that it was fashionable for doctors to

have human skeletons in their offices, but he did not like them. The reassembled human bones gave him the creeps.

"The old doc used to say he didn't feel like a doctor's office was quite right unless it had a nice skeleton hanging in it," Hornsby continued. He watched Dr. McClary arrange the books on a shelf in his glass-front bookcase before he added, "Old Doc told me—we were pretty good friends, and he used to talk to me a lot—he had to wait a long time before he could get a skeleton for his office. Just never could seem to get together enough money to buy one. Of course, there was The War and Reconstruction. Not many folks had any money then!

"It wasn't too long after The War though—along about 1868 or 1869—that Doc got his skeleton. I always wondered where he got the money to buy it. He never said."

Dr. McClary was bored with the talk of skeletons, and he was very tired. He wished his elderly, uninvited guest would take his memories of "the old doc" and go away.

"The old doc," Hornsby began. Then he paused. Maybe he was aware that Dr. McClary was not listening, that he was bored.

"Well—I know this wasn't a good time to visit. I'll come back another time, after you're settled."

"Thank you for stopping by," Dr. McClary said. He hoped his relief didn't show in his voice.

"Oh, just one more thing," Hornsby said. "This building is haunted, you know. Don't let the ghost scare you." Then he walked away.

Haunted! Dr. McClary shrugged his weary shoulders. He wanted a ghost even less than he wanted a skeleton. Since he intended to have neither, he dismissed both possibilities and went back to work.

He was adjusting his table in the examination room, placing it where it would have the best light, when, out of the corner of his eye, he saw a figure move across the waiting room.

"Who's there?" he called. Surely the long-winded visitor had not returned!

There was no reply to his question.

"Who's there?" he called again. And again there was silence. He walked quickly into the waiting room. It was deserted. So was the hall.

"Strange," he said to himself. "I was sure I saw someone go into the waiting room, someone wearing a dark robe. I must really be tired to be having such hallucinations. It's time to go home!"

He locked the door and walked home through the late April twilight.

Several days later, late one afternoon, Dr. McClary saw the figure again. He had treated his last patient and was returning a reference book to the bookcase when he saw in the glass door the reflection of someone draped in a brown garment.

Dr. McClary whirled around to accost the intruder, but no one was in the room. He searched the adjoining areas immediately, but he found nothing. He was alone in his office. And, though he was reluctant to admit it to himself, he was a little frightened. Maybe not frightened exactly but certainly uneasy.

Catching glimpses of the elusive robed figure was not his only disquieting experience. On several occasions when he was alone in his office, Dr. McClary heard a peculiar clicking noise that sounded as if someone were hitting two marbles together. Though he searched everywhere, he could not find the source of the rhythmic clicking.

As those unexplained sightings and noises continued, Dr. McClary recalled the visit of Mr. Hornsby the day he moved into his office, and he thought about his talk of skele-

21

tons and a ghost. He wished he had been more hospitable: there were questions he wanted to ask.

Then, almost as if he had conjured him up, Mr. Hornsby again stood in the doorway of the office, just as he had that first afternoon. "Well," Hornsby said, "looks like you're settled. No skeleton yet, I see."

"No," Dr. McClary answered, "no skeleton." He was tempted to add, "There may be a ghost though," but he didn't. Instead he said, "Come in and have a seat. I'd like to know more about Old Doc, as you call him."

He listened with especial interest to the stories about Old Doc's heroism during the Great Flood of 1867.

The enduring story of the flood is the account of the wreck on the East Tennessee and Georgia Railroad there in Charleston. It was a terrible tragedy.

Dr. McClary's visitor told the story of that wreck in great detail, spending a lot of time on the history of the railroad itself. It was obvious that the man was something of a railroad nut, and Dr. McClary was a bit impatient for him to get to the part he wanted to hear, the part about Old Doc.

But first Hornsby told how the railroad bridge across the Hiwassee River just north of Charleston was the first railroad bridge in Tennessee, and he gave a full description of that bridge. He told how, in 1861, four carefully chosen arsonists, all of them Union sympathizers, burned the bridge to keep it from being used by Confederate forces.

"Those were bad times," Hornsby commented. And Dr. McClary agreed.

Soon after The War ended, the bridge was rebuilt, and the railroad was in operation again. "By 1867, railroading on this line was almost back to normal," Hornsby said.

Then the rains came. Day after day it rained, a steady,

Dr. McClary saw in the glass door of his bookcase the reflection of someone draped in a brown garment.

saturating downpour. The ground was soggy and soft as a sponge. Creeks rose and dumped their muddy waters into the Hiwassee River.

Veteran river-watchers checked the rise of the Hiwassee, saw it move above the high water marks of other years, and they wondered how high it would rise on the piers of the railroad bridge before the rains ceased.

Nobody in Charleston, it seems, checked the condition of the railroad roadbed; nobody thought of the danger there until too late.

The southbound train came rolling through the rain into Charleston headed for Dalton, Georgia, and points south. The train had passed a string of small Tennessee towns—Louden, Philadelphia, Sweetwater, Mouse Creek, Athens, and Riceville—before it crossed the Hiwassee River bridge and eased toward the Charleston depot.

Between the river and the depot, sections of the roadbed gave way beneath the weight of the train. The engine and the string of cars derailed and tumbled down an embankment. Drenching rain fell on the tangled mass of wreckage. From that wreckage rose the screams and moans of passengers and crewmen.

The sounds of the crash brought almost the entire populace of Charleston to the scene. They sloshed through the downpour to free the trapped victims, to remove the injured and the dead.

The casualty list was long.

There was no hospital in Charleston, so the injured were taken into homes. A temporary morgue was set up in the depot where—much later—family members came to claim the bodies of their dead.

"Old Doc was mighty busy during that time," Dr. McClary's visitor told him. "I wasn't around then, but I've heard all about it from Old Doc. And I've heard other people

This cemetery in Charleston overlooks the railroad station.

tell about how he went from house to house taking care of the injured, folks he didn't even know, taking care of strangers. They say he worked day and night until he was so worn out he collapsed.

"It took Old Doc a long time to get his strength back. I believe he had to go spend maybe a month at a health resort somewhere. By the time he got back home, the rain had stopped, of course. The wreckage had been moved off, and the tracks had been fixed."

Dr. McClary found his mind straying. He was getting more information about the flood than he really wanted. He was wishing that Hornsby would end his stories when he suddenly became aware that the man was saying something interesting.

"...never did find that monk," he was saying.

"What monk?" Dr. McClary asked. "I guess I wasn't listening very well. I'm sorry. Please tell me about the monk."

So Mr. Hornsby told the story of the missing monk.

According to his story, a young Catholic monk, a native of Baltimore, had been aboard that ill-fated train en route to New Orleans. He never arrived at his destination, and nobody heard from him.

About a week after the wreck, his brothers and a sister came to Charleston to search for their brother. They were almost certain that he had lost his life in the accident, but he was not listed among the casualties.

Immediately after their arrival in Charleston, the brother and sister checked the identities of the dead, they inquired at all the homes where the injured had been cared for, they organized search parties to scour the countryside and to patrol the river banks where a body might surface.

During their investigation, the family found several people who remembered seeing the brown-clad monk on the train—a few of them reported having conversations with him—but nobody recalled seeing him after the wreck. He had, apparently, disappeared completely.

After the grieving family members had exhausted all hope of finding their missing brother, they prepared to return

26

to their homes in Baltimore. They delayed their home-going a few days, however, hoping that the doctor would come back to Charleston so that they could ask him about their brother. They had been told of the exhausting work the doctor had done for the victims of the wreck, and they were aware of his need for recuperative rest, but they did wish they could ask him if he had any recollection of having treated—or having seen—a young monk. Their wish was never fulfilled for they never got to talk with the doctor.

It was some time after they had returned to Baltimore before the doctor came back to Charleston. When he got home, he still looked worn and wan, and he did not care to talk about his recent experiences.

He was distressingly silent and withdrawn, residents recalled, until, several weeks after his return, he displayed a skeleton in his office. He perked up then.

Nobody knew where the skeleton came from, but everybody in Charleston knew of the doctor's pride in his new possession. He called people in from the streets to see it, and he must have said a hundred times, "I've wanted a skeleton for my office ever since I began to practice medicine, and now after all these years, my wish has been fulfilled. It's a perfect skeleton, just perfect!"

That skeleton hung in the old doctor's office as long as he practiced medicine in Charleston.

The stories of the train wreck and of the skeleton answered some questions that had been puzzling Dr. McClary, but they raised some disquieting possibilities.

Long after his guest had departed, Dr. McClary sat in his office and thought of the stories he had heard. As he sat there, quiet and alone, he heard again the distinct clicking sound, the sound he had associated with marbles being struck together. But could it be the clicking of beads? Could it? He pushed the thought out of his mind.

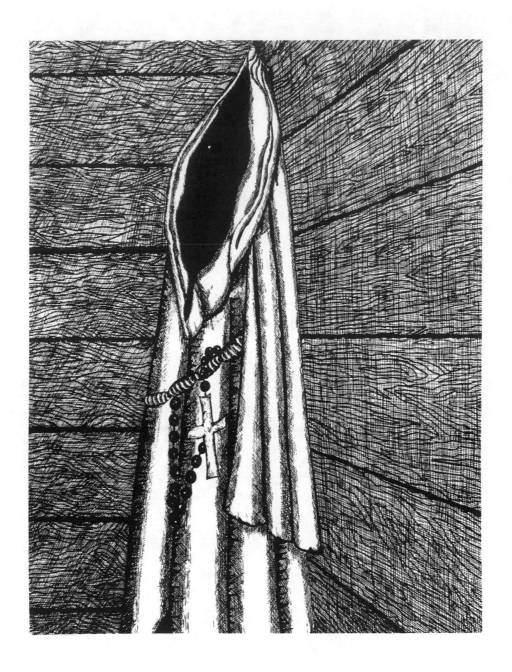

28

As he turned to leave the office, Dr. McClary saw a robed figure scurry across the room.

"Could I really be seeing a ghost?" he asked aloud. He shook his head in disbelief. Dr. McClary was a scientific man, a logical man, with nothing in his background to prepare him for accepting the reality of ghosts.

Yet he kept remembering a bit of folklore he had heard long ago. He remembered hearing that if a person's body is not given proper burial, his restless spirit will eternally haunt the area where he lost his life.

But of course, Dr. McClary told himself, he didn't believe in such superstitious nonsense.

In the years that followed, Dr. McClary and many of his patients continued to hear the clicking sounds and to see the brown-clad phantom figure in his office.

Dr. McClary continued to wonder.

In 1932 the structure where Dr. McClary had practiced medicine was demolished. Workmen tearing out the interior of the building came across two strange relics: hanging from a stud between the office walls were a monk's brown habit and an ivory rosary.

THE NOCATULA LEGEND

A wounded English officer from Fort Loudon was befriended by an Indian Chief and nursed back to health by Nocatula, daughter of the Chief. The soldier, given the name of Connestoga, "The Oak," was accepted into the tribe and married Nocatula. A jealous suitor attacked Connestoga with a knife. As he lay dying Nocatula confessed her eternal love and plunged a knife into her breast. Buried together, the Chief placed an acorn in Connestoga's hand and a hackberry in Nocatula's hand, symbolizing undying love. From these there developed two trees which stood on this spot for 150 years.

PRESENTED BY CLASSES OF 192_, 192_, 192_ AND DARISTER PATTEN

This Nocatula legend marker is on the campus of Tennessee Wesleyan College in Athens.

The Trees

The Indians left their mark on Tennessee not only by their place names that dot the state—Hiwassee, Chattanooga, Nolichucky, Hatchie, Chilhowee—but also by their legends, their stories told first around council fires and repeated in later generations on peaceful front porches.

There is, for instance, the Indian story of Reelfoot Lake in west Tennessee.

Sportsmen describe Reelfoot Lake as a hunting and fishing paradise, and if that description isn't original, it is accurate. Ducks and geese by the thousands swoop down on Reelfoot Lake to rest and feed during their migrations. Monstrous fish live in the protective shelter of rotting logs, cypress knees, and saw grass. Wild animals congregate around the shoreline.

And deadly cottonmouth moccasins sun themselves on low-hanging tree limbs.

Nobody now living remembers the time before Reelfoot

Lake was formed. Geologists and historians say it was created by the New Madrid (accent on the first syllable, please), Missouri, earthquakes between December 16, 1811, and March 15, 1812.

Indian legends tell it another way.

The tale-tellers of the Chickasaw and the Choctaw wove a story of a spurned lover, an ignored warning, a stealthy thief, and a dire punishment to explain the formation of the great lake.

According to the Indian legend, in the late summer of 1811 (though they did not then reckon time in white man's fashion), a Chickasaw chief who lived near New Madrid went wife-hunting among the Choctaws of west Tennessee. As befitted a chief, he was accompanied by a party of painted warriors.

The search for a wife was necessary because no Chickasaw maiden would marry the chief: he was clubfooted, and he walked with a funny, rolling gait. They called him Kalopin (Reelfoot), and some of the more daring maidens mimiced his peculiar hobbling—behind his back, of course. Not one of those Chickasaw maidens, not even the shy, compassionate ones who did not poke fun at the crippled chief, would consent to be his wife.

So Chief Reelfoot went wife-hunting among the neighboring Choctaws. His search took him to the village of Chief Copish. As the two chiefs sat talking, Chief Copish's daughter, Laughing Eyes, walked past. She walked with a grace and beauty such as Reelfoot had never seen before, and when she paused to smile at her father, Reelfoot knew that her name had been well chosen.

Before Laughing Eyes was out of sight, Reelfoot was pleading with her father to let her become his wife. His pleading was of no avail: Chief Copish refused to give his consent to the marriage.

Even though Reelfoot offered him bundles of choice beaver skins and promised deerhide bags filled with mussel pearls, Chief Copish would not agree to let Laughing Eyes marry Reelfoot.

Reelfoot continued stubbornly to press his suit, trying both bribery and threats in his effort to get Laughing Eyes for his own. His persistence angered Chief Copish, and the Choctaw chief ordered Reelfoot to leave. Some story-tellers say Reelfoot was literally run out of the village.

Reelfoot was angry and humiliated by the treatment he received from the Choctaw chief, but his anger and his humiliation did not erase his desire for Laughing Eyes. Day after day he was besieged by memories of her, and at night his sleep was filled with dreams of her.

Finally Reelfoot could bear the torment no longer. He determined to return to the Choctaw village and steal Laughing Eyes.

That night, instead of dreaming of the maiden he loved, his sleep was troubled by terrible dreams of earthquakes and floods, destruction and death. Reelfoot awakened trembling with fear.

He thought—feared perhaps is a better word—that he understood the meaning of the dream, but he called the wise old men to interpret it for him.

"It is an evil omen," they warned. "If you steal the maiden, our villages will be destroyed."

Reelfoot ignored the warning.

Taking a few trusted warriors with him, Reelfoot moved stealthily and speedily toward the village of Chief Copish, toward the dwelling of Laughing Eyes. It was a long journey.

They approached the village on a night when heavy clouds hid the moon and stars, and Reelfoot was grateful for the darkness. He and his warriors waited in the shadows until the inhabitants of the village were asleep. Then they stole

33

Laughing Eyes and escaped with her into the forest.

Reelfoot, delirious with joy, sent runners ahead to tell the tribe to prepare for the wedding.

"And tell the wise old men that they were wrong about my dream," Reelfoot instructed the runners. "Tell them that Laughing Eyes is mine and that the gods will smile on us."

As Reelfoot and his captured bride neared his village, he heard the tom-toms pounding the traditional rhythms of welcome, and in his imagination he saw his people gathered to dance in the great square and tasted the wedding feast they had prepared.

Suddenly the beat of the drums was drowned out by a roar louder than any noise Reelfoot had ever heard. The earth vibrated from the sound waves, and then it heaved in mighty spasms that splintered giant trees and sent them crashing down into newly formed crevices.

Then came a rushing wall of water that swallowed up the village, covered the whole countryside, and formed a great lake.

The bodies of Reelfoot and Laughing Eyes lie at the bottom of that lake, the lake called Reelfoot.

Some story-tellers say that only the old cottonmouth moccasins know where the bodies lie. Others tell of hearing the muffled beat of tom-toms on certain nights and of seeing the shadowy figure of a man reeling through the forest as though he were trying to escape from great danger.

Across the state at Athens, story-tellers recount the romantic legend of two trees and of the ghosts of long-ago lovers. The legend centers on the campus of Tennessee Wesleyan College.

The story goes back a long time, back to 1756 when the British built Fort Loudon as an outpost against the French. The British were careful to explain to their Indian allies, the Overhill Cherokee, that the fort was not a warlike gesture toward them but was designed to protect them all from mutual enemies.

With this assurance of the fort's purpose, the Overhill Cherokee accepted the garrison as a thoughtful act of friendship: it provided refuge for their women and children when the Indian braves were absent from home.

In addition, the Cherokee were fascinated by the man who had charge of constructing the fort, James William Gerald deBrahm, who was described as being "somewhat eccentric."

In addition to being an engineer, deBrahm experimented with alchemy. The Indians did not understand the purpose of the chemical concoctions created by deBrahm (some of his associates said deBrahm did not understand them either), but they found the seething, foaming liquids amazing, and when his chemical compounds produced foul odors or thick smoke, they laughed aloud.

The Indians believed that their friend deBrahm was putting on a show solely for their amusement, and often he was. He enjoyed seeing their reactions to his tricks of magic.

No Indian watched deBrahm's tricks with more interest than did Attakulla-Kulla or Little Carpenter, the great conjurer of the Cherokee. He taught the engineer-alchemist some of his Indian magic, and in return deBrahm explained some of the simple chemical reactions to the Indian. The two men enjoyed each other and respected each other.

Friendship between the British and the Overland Cherokee ended in February, 1760, when the Indians laid siege to the fort. For some time the Cherokee had been alarmed by the growing white encroachment on their lands. Acts of violence by some of the new white settlers turned the alarm into hatred, and the siege of Fort Loudon began.

The people inside the stockade held out for six months before hunger, illiness, and desperation forced their surrender. No food remained inside the fort—even the dogs and horses had been slaughtered and eaten.

In accepting the surrender, the Cherokee agreed to provide the starving people with food, and they also guaranteed safe passage for the survivors to Fort Prince George.

The first day of their march toward Fort Prince George, the group covered fifteen miles, and at nightfall they camped near Cane Creek.

Just at dawn, the camp was attacked by Indians, and thirty persons were killed (twenty-three privates, four officers, and three women). The other members of the party were made prisoners.

Among those prisoners was a young white woman whose husband had been killed in the attack. The woman begged that the life of her little son and her own life be spared.

Chief Attakulla-Kulla, for so long a friend of the white people, stepped forward and claimed the woman and the child as his prisoners. He treated them kindly, and some time later the woman became his wife.

To the couple was born a daughter, Nocatula Cooweena, also called Weena, who became the pet of the tribe.

Nocatula grew up to be a beautiful maiden, and many braves tried to win her heart. Among her suitors was Mocking Crow, a boastful brave whom Nocatula liked least of all.

Mocking Crow brought presents to Nocatula and to her father, he demonstrated his prowess as an athlete and as a hunter, he spoke of his powerful family, and he publicly boasted that Nocatula would surely be his bride. But Nocatula despised the cocky Mocking Crow and haughtily spurned his proposals of marriage.

A British soldier wounded in the battle of King's Mountain was nursed back to health by Princess Nocatula, and they fell in love.

36

Mocking Crow left the village, but he steadfastly proclaimed that Nocatula would one day be his bride.

Not long after this event, Chief Attakulla-Kulla and several Indians were on a hunt when they came upon a young British soldier lying near death in the forest. The soldier had been wounded in the Battle of King's Mountain (October 7, 1780) and had crawled away to hide so that he would not be captured.

The Indians carried the gravely wounded soldier to their village, where Nocatula nursed him back to health.

The two, the Indian princess and the British infantryman, fell deeply in love.

As soon as he had regained his strength, the soldier and Nocatula went together to ask Attakulla-Kulla's permission to marry. The chief admired and trusted the white warrior, and he was aware of the happiness he had brought to his beloved Nocatula, so he gave them his blessing.

After their marriage, the soldier was received into the tribe and was given the name Connestoga, meaning Oak. It was a proud name, just as the oak is a proud tree.

One day soon after their marriage, Connestoga bade Nocatula goodbye and went off on a hunt with some of his new Indian brothers.

Connestoga was stalking a deer, moving noiselessly behind the animal, when he heard a rustle in the bushes close by. Before he could defend himself, Mocking Crow jumped on him and thrust a knife into his throat.

Connestoga's companions heard the scuffle and rushed to his rescue, but they were too late. One of them, the fleetest one, ran to the village to fetch Nocatula.

Connestoga was still alive when Nocatula reached him, but his life was ebbing fast. Nocatula knelt beside her husband, holding his hand and stroking his face and begging him to live. "I cannot live without you," the distraught maiden cried again and again.

As Connestoga drew his final breath, Nocatula raised the same bloody knife that had stabbed him and plunged it into her own heart.

Nocatula and Connestoga were dead when Chief Attakulla-Kulla reached the scene. After he had recited the age-old prayers and laments for the dead, he said to his braves, "Do not move their bodies. They shall be buried where they died."

Then he knelt and placed an acorn in the hand of Connestoga. In Nocatula's hand he put a hackberry seed. Their friends covered the bodies of the lovers with earth from the forest.

As time passed, the seeds sprouted, and the trees, the oak and the hackberry, grew tall and straight.

"It is a good omen," the Indians said. "The gods are pleased."

Years later, a college (now Tennessee Wesleyan) was built on the site, but the trees were not disturbed. Their story, the story of the lovers, was told to each group of students who came to the college, and the trees, naturally, became a trysting place for campus lovers.

The hackberry and the oak flourished side by side until 1945 when, after 165 years, the hackberry became diseased and had to be cut down. The oak began to wither, and it had to be removed five years later.

A metal tablet now marks the site where the trees, the lovers' trees, stood.

Some students at Tennessee Wesleyan have told of seeing shadowy figures near the spot where the trees grew. Others have told of hearing soft voices near the spot.

Is it the sighing of the wind in nearby trees, or is it the voice of an Indian maiden whispering, "I love you"?

Large white oak near Surgoinsville. Tradition had it that the murdered family was camping under this tree when Murrell's murderers came upon them.

Long Dog

"Got to grease that squeaking wheel tomorrow," the wagon driver said to his wife. "Don't think I can stand to hear it complaining another two miles! Should have stopped and greased it this afternoon, but there wasn't time; dark has already caught us as it is, and I don't know how far we have to go before we find a settlement or a campsite."

His wife, sitting on the hard wagon seat beside him, tried to ease his anxiety (she was a wise wife who understood him well and knew that, though he spoke of a noisy wagon wheel, his real concern was to find shelter for the night) by saying, "The squeaking isn't bad. I don't mind it. Listen. It seems to be saying, 'New home. New home. New home.' It's nice."

She turned around and called to their son in the back of the wagon, "Don't you like it, Alex? You hear the wheel talking about our new home in Tennessee, don't you?"

Alex didn't answer. He leaned his head against a cowhide trunk and pretended to be asleep.

"The boy is asleep. Must be plumb worn out," Alex's mother whispered to her husband. "Maybe the squeaking wheel just lulled him off to sleep. He must like it, too."

Alex didn't like the noise, didn't like it at all. He pulled his knit cap down over his ears, and then he covered them with his hands, but still he heard the rhythmic squeak of the wheel repeating and repeating, "Long Dog. Long Dog. Long Dog." Alex was frightened.

He had been listening—how many hours ago? how many miles ago?—when a man had warned his father, "If you're on the road at night, be on the lookout for Long Dog. He never has hurt anybody as I know of, but he sure has scared a lot of folks traveling along near Surgoinsville after dark! He's a ghost dog, you know."

Alex's father had laughed, as though he knew the stranger were joking. The stranger didn't laugh though, Alex noticed, and something about the look in the man's eyes made Alex uneasy.

The boy wanted to know more about Long Dog, but he was too timid to ask questions. He hoped his father would ask the questions that tumbled around in his mind, but his father did not appear to be interested or concerned about the stranger's warning. He stopped only long enough to get water for the horses and information about the trail ahead, not long enough to inquire about a ghost dog.

So Alex sat in the back of the wagon and listened to the wheel grind out the fearsome warning, "Long Dog. Long Dog. Long Dog." The monotony of the sound was hypnotic, and, though he fought sleep, Alex nodded.

He waked suddenly as the wagon jolted over a big rock. He heard his father cursing the rock and the darkness, and he heard his mother say reassuringly, "We can't be far from Surgoinsville."

42

Alex stretched and tried to find a more comfortable position in the wagon.

Then he saw Long Dog.

Loping down the dark road behind the wagon came the biggest dog Alex had ever seen. The dog wasn't so tall—he was long, long and lithe and glowing.

"Papa! Papa!" Alex shouted. "It's Long Dog!"

Years later people near Surgoinsville began telling of seeing a huge, luminous dog who loped beside wagons traveling that road at night.

His parents turned around to comfort Alex about what was obviously a bad dream, and they, too, saw the animal coming toward them. Long Dog, running with a swift grace, had almost caught up with the wagon. His sleek body shone in the dark like the brilliance of reflected moonlight.

"Get away from here!" Alex's father shouted. "Get away, I say!"

The phantom dog paid no heed. He ran along by the wagon for a little piece, and then he reared up so he could look over the side. He didn't try to get into the wagon, just looked all around. He acted as if he were trying to see who was riding in the clattering vehicle. He didn't make a sound, not a sound.

The horses, sensing a strange presence, bolted and raced through the darkness. Alex's father strained back on the reins, locked the brake, and shouted to his frightened horses to halt their runaway pace.

"Whoa, now! Whoa!" he urged his team. "Hold on! Hold tight!" he called to his wife and son. For the moment, he was too busy trying to calm his horses and take care of his family to pay attention to Long Dog.

Alex braced himself against a heavy trunk in the wagon bed, and he squeezed his eyes tightly shut. Finally he felt the wagon slow almost to a stop, and he heard his father say, "It's all right now."

Quickly Alex climbed up to the front of the wagon and edged onto the seat between his parents. They all three looked behind them. Long Dog was squatting on his haunches back down the road a piece, just sitting there watching the wagon. The dog looked lonesome, Alex thought, and pitiful, too.

Alex began to cry, the first tears he had shed since they had left their home in the Carolinas. His mother pulled him to her, holding him close. His father reached over and tousled his hair and then let his strong hand remain on his head a moment, long enough to give Alex a feeling of reassurance and of blessing.

"Don't be scared," his mother said. Alex wasn't scared, not any more. He didn't know why he was crying except that his sadness was somehow mixed up with a strange ghost dog.

Later, when they finally reached Surgoinsville, his father told men there of their encounter with the luminous dog and of the runaway horses. Alex was afraid his father might tell about his tears and the men might think he was a sissy or a coward, but his father made no mention of the crying.

"That was Long Dog all right," one of the listeners said. "Lots of travelers have seen Long Dog along that stretch of road. I've seen him myself more than once." And he told the story of Long Dog, the story Alex had been wanting to hear.

As do many Tennessee tales, the story of Long Dog involves John Murrell, the notorious outlaw of the frontier.

It seems that back when Murrell was terrorizing the countryside with his bold robberies and his brutal murders, back in the late 1820s and early 1830s, a family was passing through east Tennessee on the way to a new home near Nashville.

They made camp for the night beneath a spreading white oak tree between Kingsport and Surgoinsville. While they were sleeping, Murrell and his gang (depraved men, all) fell upon the travelers and killed them. Murrell even strangled the faithful hound dog that tried to protect the family.

Some years later, possibly after Murrell had been imprisoned for his crimes, settlers traveling the old stage route to Nashville via Bristol, Rogersville, and Knoxville began to tell of seeing a mighty peculiar dog, a ghost dog, along the way.

The dog, they said, would come out of the thick shadows of a white oak tree near Surgoinsville, and he would run

45

along beside their wagons, run without making a sound. Every now and then the dog would leap up on a wagon and sniff around.

"The dog acts like he's hunting for somebody he thinks a heap of," they said.

"What does he look like? Well, he sure doesn't look like any natural dog. He's long, more than twice as long as any dog you've ever seen. I'd say he's as long as a plow line. And he shines in the dark. It's sort of like he had maybe a dozen lanterns inside him shining through his skin. Or maybe it's like he's made out of a big hunk of foxfire. It's scary looking, all right."

All of the travelers who encountered the ghost dog told almost identical stories. Not everybody believed the stories.

One of the doubters was young Marcus Hamblen, a husky eighteen-year-old who lived with his family near Surgoinsville.

"A ghost dog! If I ever saw such a glowing critter, I'd kill him and skin him and nail his hide up on the side of the barn. Or maybe I'd cut him up and use all the glowing light to go 'coon hunting on dark nights," Hamblen boasted. He didn't believe in ghosts of any kind.

Not long after he had made that boast, Marcus Hamblen (Hamblen County was named for his family) was walking home from a frolic one dark night. As he neared an old white oak tree, the ghost dog came trotting out of the shadows toward him.

Marcus snatched a rail from the fence beside the road. "Come on, old Long Dog! I'll kill you dead!" he warned.

Long Dog never slowed up, just came trotting right on toward Hamblen.

When the dog got close enough, Hamblen drew back

Marcus ran as fast as he could, and Long Dog ran right beside him.

47

with the fence rail and hit Long Dog as hard as he could.

The rail went clean through the luminous dog.

Hamblen forgot all his boasting. He dropped the rail and ran. Long Dog ran right along by him. Hamblen ran faster. So did Long Dog. Hamblen speeded up. So did Long Dog.

Hamblen ran until he didn't have a bit of breath left. He stumbled and sprawled out in the road. Long Dog squatted on his haunches right beside Hamblen and waited.

As soon as his breath and strength returned, Hamblen got up and ran again. Long Dog ran right along beside him. They ran down the road side by side, Long Dog adjusting his pace to Hamblen's, until Hamblen succumbed to exhaustion again.

Long Dog waited patiently beside the prostrate youth. When Hamblen caught his breath, off they went again.

This strange race kept up until Hamblen and Long Dog reached a particular spot in the road where, observers said, Long Dog always disappeared. That's what happened then: Long Dog completely vanished. One minute he was trotting along beside Hamblen; the next minute he was gone.

Hamblen stumbled home. He was considerably shaken ·by the experience.

That wasn't the last time Marcus Hamblen saw Long Dog, but it was the last time he ever tried to kill the ghost dog or to run away from him. In fact, as time passed, Hamblen grew fond of Long Dog and looked forward with pleasure to their infrequent encounters near the oak tree on the road to Surgoinsville.

Many people through the years saw that ghost dog, Long Dog, but probably nobody ever felt as friendly toward him as Marcus Hamblen did, and nobody ever told stories about him better than Hamblen did. Hamblen used to end his stories by saying, "Long Dog didn't mean any harm. He never tried to hurt anybody though he did scare a lot of folks. That old ghost dog was just out there trying to find his murdered master. He must have loved his master an awful lot. I hope he found him—somewhere."

It has been a good many years since anybody up in that part of Tennessee has seen Long Dog. Maybe the road has changed or maybe people drive by too fast now. Or maybe Long Dog has been reunited with his master, the way Marcus Hamblen hoped he would be.

In 1901 the old New Hope Missionary Church in the Big Springs community was torn down. A new church was built nearby.

The Barrel Of Sin

The revival at the New Hope Missionary Baptist Church was nearly over.

For more than a week families in the Big Springs community of Rutherford County had gathered nightly at the small rural church for the annual ritual of spiritual renewal. The worshippers who lived close to the church walked to the services. Others rode to the church on horseback or jolted over the rocky roads in buggies and mule-drawn wagons.

While the women and children went into the church to choose their seats, the men loitered outside to tie their animals to the long hitching poles beneath the trees and to brag on their crops, tell a few stories, or discuss the weather, speaking in subdued tones as befitted a churchyard. Not until the congregation began singing the opening hymn did most of the men break off their conversations and join their families inside the sultry building.

"Hope he don't preach about Hell again tonight—it's

51

already too hot inside the church house," a sweating farmer whispered. He was standing inside the door and looking around to see where his wife was sitting.

"Amen!" his companion answered, ever so softly.

It was hot. The string of bright, rainless days had dried up gardens and had lowered the water level in some wells so drastically that the ropes on the buckets had to be lengthened.

There was even some uneasiness that, unless rains came soon, the creek would be so low the baptisings would have to be postponed. Ever since the church was established in 1846, baptism of new converts had always been held the Sunday after the revival closed. But now the creek was so shallow that immersion would be impossible.

It would be a pity to have to put off the baptisms: an unusually large number of people had asked to be received into the fellowship of the church.

Among the first converts to join the church was Miss Bertha. On the second verse of the invitational hymn the very first night of the revival, she squeezed past the people on her bench, walked down the aisle, and gave her hand to the waiting preacher. It wasn't Miss Bertha's first trip down that aisle: she joined every summer.

The thing was, she was a faithful joiner of the Methodist Church, too. The Methodists generally had their revival early in the summer, and Miss Bertha was always right there to receive the right hand of Christian fellowship when the preacher announced that the doors of the Methodist Church were open.

Then eight or ten weeks later when the Baptists had their revival, she would switch allegiance and ask for membership in the Baptist fellowship. So actually Miss Bertha's joining didn't really count (it was widely felt, however, that she was more Baptist than Methodist, even though her joinings were equal in number, since she stayed Baptist all through the fall, winter, and spring until the Methodist revival in June), but she would have to be baptised—again—since she had requested it.

Miss Bertha and all the rest of the new members would have to wait awhile for their baptisings—unless the rains came soon.

There was lightning that night, though not the kind that promised rain. It was heat lightning, flashing about the sky, far off.

Inside the church, the heat was oppressive. No breeze came through the open windows. The only stirring of air came from the dozens of fans—palmettoes, turkey tails, folding fans painted with scenes of faraway beaches, stiff cardboard ovals embossed with colorful advertisements, heavy paper creased into accordian pleats—held in dozens of swaying hands.

Babies, uncomfortable in the heat, whimpered until they went to sleep in their mothers' arms. As they fell asleep, their mothers, one by one, tiptoed to the front of the church and gently laid the babies on a pallet spread just to the left of the pulpit. The pallet that night was a quilt of the bear paw pattern, a quilt described by its owner as "most wore out, but soft for babies to rest on."

Older children, overcome by sleep, stretched out on the bare benches—if there was room—or leaned over and rested their heads on their mothers' laps.

Neither the restless stirring of the babies on the pallet (occasionally a mother would leave her seat and go up to pacify a wakeful infant) nor the uncoordinated movements of the fans distracted the preacher. He was preaching about Hell, and he was warming up to his subject.

He was in the midst of bellowing a fearful description of the never-ending tortures of the unsaved when the services were interrupted in a most peculiar and spectacular way.

A barrel, spurting thick smoke at each end, appeared from nowhere and rolled clattering and smoking right up to the pulpit. It looked like the preacher had conjured up a living sample of Hell.

Mothers ran to the front of the church to snatch their babies from the pallet. Fathers dragged groggy children outside the church. Some worshippers climbed over the benches and jumped out the windows. The preacher pushed past the stampeding choir and escaped through the back door. (Later he said he was trying to clear a safe exit for the singers, but nobody else remembered it quite that way.)

Horses and mules, as terrified as their owners, broke from their tethers and ran away into the darkness.

After everybody was safely outside, after the screaming and crying and praying for deliverance had subsided, a group of the bravest men ventured back into the church to investigate.

A haze of dark smoke hung over the front of the church, but there was no barrel in the building. The men searched everywhere inside the church (there was only one room, so there weren't many places to look) for the clattering barrel or for its charred remains, but they found nothing.

Then they looked outside: under the church, on top of the church, around the church, in the woods, in the graveyard. There was no barrel. It had vanished completely. Only intangibles, a smoky haze and frightening memories, remained.

"Nothing here. Whatever it was has gone. We might as well go home, too," the spokesman for the group said.

So they walked home, all of them, keeping close togeth-

It frightened the horses tied to the hitching rails outside the church. They bolted and ran, and all the worshippers had to walk home.

54

er and not talking much.

By the next day, news of the smoking, clanking barrel that had broken up the meeting at the New Hope Missionary Baptist Church had spread all over Rutherford and Cannon counties. People who had been there told of the events again and again, tried to answer the questions they were asked, or became silent when confronted by rude doubters.

The accounts of the event were not alike in every detail. Some witnesses said the barrel made a circuit around the outside of the church before it entered and rolled up the aisle to the pulpit. Others testified that the barrel made its first appearance at the rear of the church where it bumped and clanked toward the pulpit. They all agreed, however, that the barrel appeared without warning, that smoke poured from each end, and that it made a terrible racket, like it might have been filled with trace chains and plow points that clattered together as it rolled along.

Search for the barrel or for some tangible evidence of its strange visitation continued for several days, but nothing was ever found. After the smoky haze drifted away, only the memories remained.

Yet people going to the church (curiosity drew hundreds of visitors to the site) became uncomfortably aware that something—some powerful force, some unseen presence, some hidden menace—had come to New Hope.

Pretty soon there was widespread talk that New Hope Church was haunted.

There was talk, too, first whispered and later spoken boldly, about the cause of the haunting: the restless, tormented spirit of a murdered man was seeking retribution.

According to the story, a resident of the Big Springs area, a highly respected man, had killed a pack peddler who stopped by the man's house for shelter from a sudden summer storm. Motive for the murder was never clear, but the murderer was reported to have robbed his victim, stuffed his body into a barrel, weighted the barrel with scrap iron, and thrown it into a swift stream.

Nobody provided positive proof of such a brutal deed, but there were those in the community who declared the story could be verified "if you just looked in the right place."

The murderer, the story continued, was tormented by the memory of what he had done (he was basically a good, kind man), and he tried to salve his conscience by giving the stolen money to the church, New Hope.

The congregation had been meeting in homes in the community for several months while an effort was underway to build a church. Land had been acquired, labor promised, and money for the building was being collected. This was in the late 1840s, a dozen or more years before the incident of the barrel.

The generous and unexpected gift of the murderer (though no one suspected him of evil-doing at the time) made the building possible.

"So you see, sinful money went into the church house. Sinful money. That's the meaning of that barrel with its smoke and racket. It was purely a barrel of sin," a deacon explained.

Maybe that was the explanation. Maybe not. But other strange things began to happen around New Hope Church.

People passing the church at night began to tell of seeing weird lights darting about, glowing balls of brightness that chased them down the road.

Other people told of hearing a baby crying at the deserted church. The baby would cry, they said, until passersby walked to a certain tombstone in the graveyard and touched it. Then the crying would stop. Nobody could ever find where the crying came from.

There were also reports of a headless man who would

57

appear out of the darkness and try to get into passing wagons or to climb up behind riders on horseback.

They say that one night, long after midnight, the headless man appeared to a local fiddler. The fiddler had been playing for a dance at a house not far away (he had been warned many times that fiddling and dancing were works of the Devil), and he was taking a short cut home through the churchyard. He was whistling, not to keep up his courage but because he was happy, when right in front of him he saw the headless man.

The fiddler started running. So did the headless man. The fiddler tripped over a root and stumbled headfirst to the ground. The fall knocked the breath out of him. When his head cleared, a quick survey assured the fiddler that the headless man was gone. But his precious fiddle was broken to smitherines.

Then there is the tale they told of the man who was dared to spend the night in the church. He was a brave man, not the kind who would take a dare, so he went to the church and let himself in. The church was no more scary than any other dark, isolated building is, so the man stretched out on a bench up near the front and went to sleep.

Along about midnight he waked up. Stiffness from sleeping on the hard bench may have awakened him, or it may have been the bright moonlight shining through the window by his head. He got up from the bench, stretched, and started to walk across the aisle. Suddenly he was surrounded by a cluster of moaning, ghostly figures.

Brave though he was, the man wanted to bolt from the church, but the ghosts blocked his exit. What could he do? He had nothing to defend himself with.

In desperation, he snatched up the collection plates and started toward the figures, waving the plates in front of him.

The ghosts disappeared instantly.

58

To be truthful, that incident probably did not happen at New Hope. It is the kind of tale that makes good listening, and it may not have happened anywhere.

Enough strange things did happen at New Hope though—appearances of the headless man and the darting lights and the crying baby and such—that there was a marked decline in the size of the congregation.

Finally the leaders decided to tear the old church down. The congregation was not disbanded: a new church was built right across the road.

The hauntings ceased.

Gradually people quit talking about the mysterious barrel and the other ghostly occurrences there. As years passed, the events were almost forgotten except by a few old story-tellers who passed the tales from generation to generation.

New Hope Missionary Baptist Church is an active, thriving church now. There's preaching there every Sunday and prayer meeting on Wednesday nights.*

*The ghost story "The Barrel of Sin" in this volume is adapted from Lourene Salmon's "The Tale of the Mysterious Barrel and other 'Haint' Tales Collected in Big Springs" in the *Tennessee Folklore Society Bulletin*, XXXVII, No. 3 (September, 1971), 59-72. By permission of the Tennessee Folklore Society, owner of coypright, and Lourene Salmon.

Does the ghost of Meriwether Lewis roam restlessly along the Natchez Trace where the dark legend began the night he died in 1809?

The Dark Legend

Does the ghost of Meriwether Lewis roam restlessly along the Natchez Trace where, as the monument on his grave says, "his life of romantic endeavor and lasting achievement came tragically and mysteriously to its close"? Is there sometimes, just before dawn, the sound of a long-handled gourd dipper scraping against an empty water bucket? Are Lewis' final words, "It is so hard to die," whispered over and over until they are caught up and lost in the rustling of leaves and the sleepy stirrings of birds?

Official records of the Natchez Trace mention no such ghostly occurrences, but all along the old road, that wilderness pathway, the dark legend endures.

The dark legend began, perhaps, on October 11, 1809, the night that Lewis died. Perhaps it had begun earlier, stalking the red-haired explorer across a continent—along the rapids of unnamed rivers, through frozen mountain passes, to the cliffs of the Pacific—delaying, waiting, hesitating, and

61

finally choosing a lonely Indian stand in middle Tennessee as spawning ground for the Lewis legend.

There beside the Natchez Parkway, not far from Gordonsburg, Lewis' burial site is marked by a circular granite column rising from a square base of native stones. The grassy plot around the marker slopes toward the old roadbed of the Trace, the deep shade of hardwoods, the playgrounds and campsites of the Meriwether Lewis Park.

Those hardwoods, or others like them, were there that stormy, sultry October afternoon when Lewis rode up to Grinder's stand to find shelter for the night. Lewis was thirty-five years old, governor of the Louisiana Territory, hero of the Lewis and Clark expedition to explore the West, friend and confidant of Thomas Jefferson—and he was a troubled, frustrated man.

Fate, the same fate which had spared his life during hazardous years of Western explorations, guided Lewis to Grinder's stand on the Natchez Trace, led him to the lonely outpost where death waited and where the dark legend began to grow.

Looking back, the circumstances surrounding the hero's death appear marked by a mystical sort of strangeness. An undiagnosed illness, an abrupt change in a journey's route, a chance companion along the Trace, a violent thunderstorm, frightened horses, errant servants wove a net of tragedy that snared Lewis in its meshes.

It happened this way:

In September, 1809, Lewis, then governor of the Louisiana Territory, set out from his St. Louis headquarters for Washington, D.C., where he intended to challenge the Washington bureaucracy. Lewis' immediate concern with that bureaucrary was his outrage over a small expense account (a draft for less than $20.00 to cover costs of stationery) which government clerks had failed to approve, but his resentment and anger ran deeper, deep enough to prod him into taking the long and uncomfortable trip to the nation's capital.

Lewis also had a second purpose, a pleasanter one, for his trip: he intended to take along papers and documents from his western explorations to be edited and published in Washington or Philadelphia. He also looked forward with eagerness to a reunion with his family and friends.

So on a September day in 1809, Governor Lewis and two companions set out from St. Louis to Washington. John Pernia, described as a Creole derelict whom Lewis had befriended, and a Negro slave known as Captain Tom pushed their flatboat away from the St. Louis landing as Lewis waved farewell to a small group of friends who had come to see him off.

It was Lewis' plan to drift down the Mississippi to New Orleans where he, his servants, and his papers would get passage on a boat bound for the eastern seaboard. The leisurely trip down river would give him respite from the strain of his duties as governor (so many problems!) and would also give him time to work on organizing and rewriting some of the reports of his expedition.

By the time the voyagers reached Fort Pickering near Chickasaw Bluffs (the present site of Memphis), Lewis was ill. Some historians say he had been drinking heavily. Others attribute the illness to a debilitating digestive upset. Still others speculate that his grievances with Washington and the frustrations of governing a new territory had rendered him emotionally unbalanced.

For whatever reason, Lewis' old friend Gilbert Russell, then commanding officer at Fort Pickering (a post Lewis himself had held in 1797), persuaded him to rest there until he recovered. After about six days, Captain Russell later reported, Lewis was "perfectly restored in every respect and ready for travel."

However, his plans for the journey had changed. Instead of continuing down river, Lewis decided to get horses and make the trip overland, going northeastward through Tennessee to the nation's capital. Though more strenuous than the journey by water, the overland route would be quicker, and Lewis had a gnawing feeling of urgency to complete his mission.

This need for haste was born and nurtured at Fort Pickering where, during his days of convalescence, Lewis had heard disquieting reports that war between the United States and England could begin at any moment. British warships were already lurking in coastal waters, he was informed, and attacks on U.S. shipping were expected. Fearful that his accounts of the Lewis and Clark Expedition might fall into enemy hands and be lost forever, Lewis mapped out an overland route to Washington and made arrangements for provisions for the journey.

A new companion, Captain James Neely, agent to the Chickasaw Indians, insisted on accompanying Lewis and his servants. Neely knew the country well, and perhaps Lewis welcomed his companionship.

Neely was obviously impressed by Lewis' fame and popularity, and, being ambitious, considered it a fortunate opportunity that he should be closely associated with the great man. He intended to take every advantage of that opportunity.

The four riders with their pack ponies crossed the Tennessee River and struck the Natchez Trace, probably not far from the present town of Waynesboro. The Trace was no easy thoroughfare, but it was a recognizable pathway through the wilderness—and it did promise comfort and safety at Nashville.

The fall of 1809 was oppressively hot, and the travelers welcomed the violent thunderstorms which exploded through the heavens on the afternoon of October 10. Though the torrents of rain drenched them, the storms brought relief from the sultry heat.

The storms brought problems, too. The intensity of the lightning and thunder, crashing to earth and rumbling through the forest, frightened the pack horses, and the animals stampeded.

Pernia and Captain Tom (the slave) may have shared the animals' fright or they may have been huddled in a temporary, makeshift shelter. In any event, they neglected their duty and permitted two pack horses to run away. The horses were carrying cases of Lewis' papers.

This event naturally upset Lewis: he had made the arduous overland journey to prevent any possibility of losing his precious papers, and now he was losing them because of the skittishness of horses and the neglect of servants.

When a search failed to locate either missing horses or missing servants, Captain Neely offered to go back to look for the strays. He gave Lewis directions for reaching Grinder's stand, an unimposing cluster of log buildings recently erected to provide accommodations for travelers, and he turned back along the way they had come.

Thus Lewis was alone when he arrived, late in the afternoon of October 10, at Grinder's stand. The rain had stopped, and a cloud-banked western sky promised a colorful sunset.

Lewis' halloos brought Mrs. Grinder and two small children to the door of one of the cabins. Mr. Grinder was off hunting, but she expected him soon, the woman told Lewis. She rather reluctantly permitted him to make arrangements for lodging for himself and his absent companions.

Those companions had not arrived by suppertime—and neither had Mr. Grinder—so Lewis shared the meal with Mrs. Grinder and the children.

By bedtime, the two servants had arrived at Grinder's stand, but whether or not they had the missing horses in tow is not known. They brought in, at Lewis' request, his bearskin and buffalo robes, both used on his western adventure, and spread them on the floor for him to sleep on. Lewis had had enough experience with frontier inns to know that he would sleep better and be safer from attacks by vermin if he slept on the floor than if he occupied the bed.

Exactly what happened next is not clear. Mrs. Grinder gave this account of the events:

Lewis was distraught all evening, alternately pacing back and forth while he muttered to himself, and then sitting calmly by the doorway, smoking his pipe and commenting on the pleasantness of the evening.

His behavior upset her, she said, so she kept the children with her in the kitchen, where she sat up all night.

Sometime after midnight, Mrs. Grinder said, she heard a pistol shot and heard Lewis wail, "O, Lord!" Then there was another shot.

In a few minutes, she heard Lewis at the kitchen door begging to be let in. She was afraid, Mrs. Grinder said, and stayed silent behind the bolted door. Through the cracks between the logs (the cabins were unchinked), she watched the shadowy figure stumble around the yard, heard him scrape a gourd dipper against the bottom of an empty water bucket in a futile effort to assuage his thirst, heard him moan, "It is so hard to die!"

Through it all, she said, she stayed inside the kitchen.

When the sky lightened with the coming of dawn, Mrs. Grinder sent the children to the barn to summon Lewis' servants. Mrs. Grinder and the servants entered Lewis' room where they found him lying on the bed. Part of his forehead was blown away, and he had a gaping wound in his side. He begged Pernia to relieve him of his suffering. Death came

His death was called a suicide, but his friends never believed he would take his own life, and recent historians have called it murder.

soon after dawn to do what the servant, through tenderness or cowardice, could not do.

By mid-morning, the other characters in the drama, Grinder and Captain Neely, arrived. Grinder, long overdue, returned from his hunt and was told by his wife what had happened. It was her first recital of a story which she told so often in later months that hardly a word or an inflection or a facial expression changed as she related the events of that fateful night.

(Listeners who heard her recital later wondered about certain aspects of the story: much of it appeared too detailed, too pat, as though she had been carefully rehearsed about what to say.)

Captain Neely cantered up about mid-morning, tied his horse, and was duly informed by Mrs. Grinder of what had transpired. The officer controlled his shock and grief sufficiently to write a letter immediately to Thomas Jefferson informing him of Lewis' "suicide." His own overnight absence was never explained.

There are other accounts of Lewis' death. One report says that his throat was slashed, and another tells that his body was found in the woods some distance from the stand, and that he had been shot in the back.

Certainly not everyone accepted Captain Neely's instant verdict of suicide. Men who had known Lewis during the harrowing months of exploration in the West, particularly Captain Clark, refused to believe that a man so brave and so self-reliant would ever take his own life.

Suspicion pointed to Grinder with robbery as a motive. Lewis, witnesses at the scene said, had only twenty-five cents on his person when he died. It is hardly logical, friends said, that he would have set out on such a long and expensive journey with so little cash. The gold he was believed to have been carrying was never found.

Grinder was, during the course of the investigation, arrested and charged with murder. However, there was no real evidence against him, and he was released.

Soon afterwards, Grinder left the stand he had so recently acquired and moved to western Tennessee where he reportedly bought for cash considerable land and slaves.

Suspicion also pointed to the Creole, Pernia, who disappeared immediately after Lewis' death, supposedly returning to his native New Orleans. Lewis' watch, a distinctive timepiece given by President Jefferson, was later found in New Orleans.

Some historians have hinted at a conspiracy involving Captain Neely and highly placed but jealous and ambitious officials in St. Louis. Proof of such a conspiracy would be difficult to obtain.

Thirty years after his death, a small trunk containing Lewis' papers was shipped by unknown persons from an unknown location to his step-sister in the East.

For years, as the dark legend grew, Captain Meriwether Lewis, American hero, lay in an unmarked grave beside a lonely wilderness footpath.

Today when travelers along the Trace turn off to visit Lewis' grave and to read the inscription on the marker beside it, some of them are conscious, as visitors to the isolated spot have been through the years, of a restless presence, a vibrant force, pervading the place. They hear in the rustle of the trees a whispered, "It is so hard to die." And they wonder.

And the dark legend grows.

Strange sounds are still heard along the lonely section of the Trace where a tall shaft marks Lewis' final resting place. The Lewis marker beside it bears a historic inscription. *

MERIWETHER LEWIS
1774-1809

BENEATH THIS MONUMENT ERECTED UNDER LEGISLATIVE ACT OF THE STATE OF TENNESSEE, A.D., 1848, REPOSES THE DUST OF MERIWETHER LEWIS, A CAPTAIN IN THE UNITED STATES ARMY, PRIVATE SECRETARY TO PRESIDENT JEFFERSON, SENIOR COMMANDER OF THE LEWIS AND CLARK EXPEDITION, AND GOVERNOR OF THE TERRITORY OF LOUISIANA.

IN THE GRINDER HOUSE, THE RUINS OF WHICH ARE STILL DISCERNIBLE, 230 YARDS SOUTH OF THIS SPOT, HIS LIFE OF ROMANTIC ENDEAVOR AND LASTING ACHIEVEMENT CAME TRAGICALLY AND MYSTERIOUSLY TO ITS CLOSE ON THE NIGHT OF OCT. 11, 1809.

THE REPORT ON THE COMMITTEE APPOINTED TO CARRY OUT THE PROVISIONS OF THE MONUMENT ACT, CONTAINS THESE SIGNIFICANT STATEMENTS:

"GREAT CARE WAS TAKEN TO IDENTIFY THE GRAVE. GEORGE NIXON, ESQ., AN OLD SURVEYOR, HAD BECOME VERY EARLY ACQUAINTED WITH THE LOCALITY. HE POINTED OUT THE PLACE; BUT TO MAKE ASSURANCE DOUBLY SURE THE GRAVE WAS RE-OPENED AND THE UPPER PORTION OF THE SKELETON EXAMINED AND SUCH EVIDENCE FOUND AS TO LEAVE NO DOUBT OF THE PLACE OF INTERMENT."

A dirt road crosses the L&N tracks near Chapel Hill. A ghost light appears at this crossing—hundreds of people have seen it.

The Chapel Hill Light

Jackie Gentry stood on a crosstie and looked up the railroad track. Somewhere behind him, a discordant chorus of frogs croaked in the night.

Closer by, Jackie heard his uncle and their friend, Peewee Coursey, whispering and chuckling. Jackie knew they were talking about him and laughing at him. He kicked one of the steel rails. Then he reached down, picked up a piece of chert, and threw it into the darkness. The raucous frogs missed nary a croak.

The uncle and Peewee heard the missile whip through the bushes.

"Whatcha doing, Jackie?" his uncle called. "Trying to scare the ghost away?"

"Yeah, Jackie—What you chunking at?" Peewee asked. "You ain't getting scared, are you?"

"Let's go home," his uncle said. "We been standing around here in the dark long enough. Guess you know now there's not any ghost light. Don't know why you ever believed such a tale in the first place. We all ought to have better sense than to be out here. Let's go."

Jackie didn't reply. He reached down to get another hunk of chert, and, as he straightened up, he saw the light coming down the track toward him.

"It's coming! The light's coming!" Jackie called to his taunting companions. "Come up here on the track with me. Hurry! You can see it real good from—"

"We can see it from here in the road—it's close enough," they replied. Their teasing stopped.

As they watched, the circle of light advanced and retreated, bobbing about as though following the pattern of a traditional dance. Then it paused and swooped toward Jackie.

Just as it reached the young man, its brilliance faded. The area returned to complete darkness.

Out of the darkness came a loud thud. Jackie felt the crosstie shake beneath his feet.

Accompanying the thud came a sudden chill, a paralyzing cold that enveloped Jackie. His teeth chattered, and his skin prickled with goosebumps. For an instant he lost all power to move: an invisible force seemed to hold him immobile.

Then, as the strange force released him, Jackie whirled around in time to see the light, brilliant again, speed down the tracks and vanish in the night.

And he heard his uncle exclaim in amazement, "That light went right through Jackie! Did you see it, Peewee? It went right through him!"

"Yeah, I saw," Peewee replied slowly.

Later, when the three of them were safely at home again, they told their story of Jackie's encounter with the phantom light. The uncle didn't laugh or scoff about the light, and neither did Peewee. They didn't understand what had happened on the railroad tracks there near Chapel Hill that night, but they knew they had witnessed an awesome and strange occurrence.

Perhaps even stranger was the encounter four other young men had with the Chapel Hill light in the early 1970s.

The four Tennessee youths were out looking for excitement one night, and they decided to go investigate the light. They had, for years, heard many tales about the mysterious glowing ball often seen on the tracks near Chapel Hill, and, though they told each other they really didn't believe in such things, they thought they might as well go check it out.

They drove their car out just west of Chapel Hill to where a narrow dirt road takes a sharp and sudden incline as it crosses the L&N Railroad tracks. Instead of parking their car beside the road and walking back to stand between the steel rails, the quartet stopped their car right on the tracks. The driver left the motor running: he didn't figure they'd waste much time there.

They were sitting in the car teasing and joking about anybody foolish enough to believe in a ghost light, when they saw the light moving down the track toward them. There wasn't a sound of any kind, just that glowing ball getting closer and closer.

"Let's get out of here!" one of the boys yelled.

The driver shifted gears and slammed his foot down on the accelerator. The car didn't move. He gunned the motor. The car remained stationary.

"Let's go!" his companions urged. The light was almost upon them.

Again the driver gunned the motor. Again. Again. The car did not respond.

The light moved straight and steadily toward the stalled car. Inside the vehicle, the youths ducked to protect themselves from what seemed an inevitable collision. But there was no collision, only a diminishing in the intensity of the light.

"It's on top of the car," one of the youths whispered.

It was. An eerie, subdued glow filled the automobile.

Then the boys heard a loud thud, similar to the one Jackie Gentry had told of hearing, and the light sped away.

So did the four boys. For as the light moved away, the car lurched forward. They did not slow down until they reached the familiar and welcome lights of a filling station.

It was at this filling station, after they had told their story and had recovered from their acute fear, that one of the boys discovered rows of deep scratches down the back of the car.

Those scratches, the boys agreed, had not been there when they set out to investigate the ghost light. Where had the marks come from? Who or what had branded the car with a string of scratches there in the dark on the railroad tracks?

The four youths never found a satisfactory answer to the mystery. Nor did they ever find a logical explanation for the Chapel Hill light itself.

Jackie Gentry, Peewee, the uncle, and the four boys in the car are among scores of Tennesseans who have had strange experiences with the darting light on the railroad tracks near Chapel Hill. Next to the account of the witch who tormented the Bell family in Robertson County, no Tennessee tale of the supernatural is more widely known than is the story of the Chapel Hill ghost light. All over Tennessee there are people who say sincerely, "I've seen the Chapel Hill light. I know that story is true."

Other people, just as sincere, deny that the light is supernatural: it is the reflection of trucks' headlights bouncing off the smooth steel rails, they say. Still others attribute the light to foxfire or swamp gas, a common explanation (and often correct) for such phenomena. Complete skeptics

The light paused and swooped toward Jackie.

dismiss the story by denying the existence of the light entirely, terming it "just people's imaginations gone wild."

But the scoffers and the scientific explainers and the skeptics do not shake the testimonies of the Tennesseeans who have personally witnessed the gyrations of the ghost light.

These witnesses tell basically the same story. They tell of going, usually late at night, to a railroad crossing near Chapel Hill. They stand, facing north, between the rails, they say, and the light comes swooping down the tracks toward them. It appears from nowhere, they say, a giant, glowing ball that quickly vanishes into the darkness.

Some witnesses say the ball of light dances and cavorts around, almost as though it were playing a game of tag. Others report that the light moves unerringly forward in a straight line until it disappears from sight.

And when it disappears, the Chapel Hill light leaves behind it an aura of uneasiness, of foreboding, of fear.

The light, of course, does not appear on schedule. Months may pass without a sighting, and then there may be reports for several nights in a row from witnesses who tell of seeing the luminous globe.

But nobody who has seen the Chapel Hill light dismisses the experience casually. Nor do many of the viewers desire a repeat performance.

The light, according to one story told around Chapel Hill, is a ghostly lantern that belonged to a railroad flagman who lost his life in an accident near the spot.

It was a dark, rainy night when the accident happened, they say. Days and nights of steady rain had washed the fill from beneath a section of tracks, making it dangerous for trains to travel on.

To warn of this danger, a trainman was given a lantern, the story goes, and was told to flag down a fast freight heading south out of Nashville. As soon as he heard the train approaching, the flagman moved onto the shoulder of the tracks and began waving the lantern.

Nobody knows exactly how the accident happened, but it seems the flagman lost his footing on the wet incline, slipped, and fell into the path of the train.

His head was cut clean off, they say, and ever since that time there have been stories of the ghostly flagman looking for his head.

It is a logical, almost classical story (similar tales of headless trainmen are told in other states), but there is no record in Chapel Hill of any fatal railroad accident ever happening there.

However, there were other tragedies along those tracks, tragedies which many present-day residents of the small town recall.

Back in the late 1930s, along about 1937 or 1938, a man named Skip Adgent was struck and killed by a train at the crossing where the light is now seen.

"It wasn't long after Skip's death that folks began telling about seeing a strange light at the crossing," older residents say. "Seems like they connect the light with Skip's troubled spirit. That's what I've always heard."

Other local residents reject that story. They contend the light didn't appear until after a Mrs. Ketchum was murdered.

"That murder was an awful thing," they recall. "Just awful."

Mrs. Ketchum, mother of two young children, disappeared from her rural home near Chapel Hill in late December, 1940, according to local accounts.

At first there wasn't a big stir about her being missing. Some neighbors figured she had gone somewhere for a holiday visit, though it did seem a mite strange that she didn't take the children with her and that she didn't tell anybody

79

she planned to go off.

As days passed without anybody seeing or hearing from her, search parties were organized to look for her. Foul play, as they say, was strongly suspected.

"She must be dead," law enforcement spokesmen said, "but we can't find her body."

Suspicion of being involved in the disappearance (it could not at that point be called murder) of Mrs. Ketchum centered on a man who lived not far from her home. Gossips had linked him to the missing woman, but no open accusations or charges could be brought against him until the body was found.

Then, after the woman had been missing more than two weeks, the suspect took his own life. Many people familiar with the case were convinced that a guilty conscience had prompted his suicide.

The search was intensified. Teams of men scoured the bitter cold countryside, but nobody found a single clue. Everybody termed it a really baffling case.

In mid-January, 1941, several townspeople, discouraged by lack of progress in solving the mystery of the missing body, drove over to Shelbyville, some twenty miles away, to consult Simon Warner. Mr. Warner was a clairvoyant or fortuneteller whose amazing ability to find lost things and missing people was known all over Tennessee and neighboring states.

Mr. Warner listened to the story told by the Chapel Hill delegation. He said he had read something about the case in the Nashville papers. He thought a little while, and then he described in detail the spot where Mrs. Ketchum's body would be found. The description was so plain that some of the men recognized the place right away.

The body, frozen stiff, was found exactly where Simon Warner had said it would be. Exactly. It was hidden under a pile of brush. Warner had told about that brush pile, too.

No autopsy was performed and no cause of death was listed on the death certificate, Thomas Lawrence, long-time Chapel Hill undertaker, recalls.

Mr. Lawrence doesn't hold with stories about the ghostly light. He doesn't believe in ghosts of any kind. And he wonders why people keep coming to Chapel Hill hoping to see the light.

The light-seekers do come, though not as many of them as once invaded the little town. Interest in the light, it seems, comes in cycles. A few years ago, so many people were attracted to Chapel Hill by stories of the light that extra lawmen had to be brought in to handle the crowds, and guards were needed to protect the railroad property.

"It was rough when such big crowds converged on Chapel Hill to try to see the light," recalls Mayor Ezell Scott. "There were more people than we were able to handle—and some of them got right rowdy." He paused.

"You know," he continued, "it used to be—before the ghost light thing started—that people came to Chapel Hill to see where General Nathan Bedford Forrest was born. Now visitors aren't interested in that Confederate military genius: they just want to know about the ghost light."

Although the Memphis skyline has changed since the Brink-ley College ghost made the front pages of the Memphis papers, the Mississippi River has not.

Memphis' Great Jar Mystery

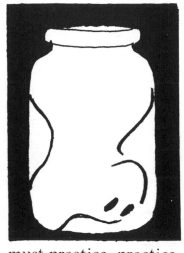

Clara Robertson hated to have to practice scales. And she hated the way her music teacher said to her, "Miss Clara, you will not play pieces—not even hymns—until you have mastered your scales. You must practice, practice, practice!"

Clara, who was thirteen, was not particularly interested in playing hymns. She did not really care about learning to play anything on the piano, not if it required the repetitious and untuneful ascending and descending of the keyboard.

However, the study of piano was required of the fifty young ladies who were privileged to attend the Brinkley Female College in Memphis. So Clara sat dutifully at the piano in the upstairs music room of the old home that housed the college, and she tried to master the hateful assignment her teacher had given her. She sat with her back rigid, as she had been taught to do, and she concentrated on holding her fingers in the graceful arc favored by her teacher.

As Clara was playing the G-major scale for the tenth

time, she looked up from the keyboard and saw a little girl, the most gruesome creature Clara had ever seen, standing near the piano. The child's eyes stared from sunken sockets, and her scraggly hair framed a face as bony as that of a skeleton. A tattered pink dress, dank and moldy, hung limply from her thin shoulders. There was a deeper pink blotch or stain on the front of that musty dress.

Clara screamed in terror and ran from the room.

The apparition followed her down the hall and into an adjoining room where Clara tried to hide in a monstrous feather bed. The strange child stood beside the bed and, to Clara's horror, reached out to touch the pillow Clara was using as a shield. Only when it seemed that Clara would go into a paroxysm of fear did the figure vanish.

Clara leapt from the bed and ran down the stairs. In the downstairs hall, she bumped into a teacher, almost knocking the startled woman down, and blurted out what had happened to her upstairs.

The commotion attracted a cluster of students to the hallway, and they listened in amazement to Clara's account of her strange encounter. Their reactions were mixed: some of them believed every word Clara said, two or three seemed on the verge of hysterics themselves, and others ridiculed Clara for telling such a big fib.

Clara, still upset, was taken home where she told her parents about seeing the pathetic phantom. Her parents listened patiently, but they felt sure that Clara had either been the victim of a school joke or that her imagination had run wild. So when Clara declared, "I will not ever go back to that place!" her father said calmly, "Of course you will go back. You will return to school tomorrow morning. Nothing will happen to you."

Clara's father, J. R. Robertson, was one of Memphis' leading attorneys, and his words were persuasive at home as well as in the courtroom.

So Clara returned to school the next day. And if she spent more time repeating her story of the ghostly visitation than she did studying her lessons, at least she was there. And, just as her father predicted, nothing unusual happened.

The following day, however, the little girl ghost appeared again. Clara and two other pupils were in the practice room together, and all three of them saw the child in the musty pink dress. All three pupils fled from the room.

This time it took powerful persuasion on the part of her father to get Clara to go back to Brinkley's Female College, but she did return.

There were four uneventful days, and the young ladies at the school had almost stopped talking about the ghost. Then, exactly one week after she had first appeared to Clara (that initial appearance was on February 21, 1871), the grisly figure returned. As on the two previous occasions, Clara was in the practice room when she saw the child. Again Clara fled in fright.

On this occasion, she met Miss Jackie Boone, one of her teachers, in the hallway. Miss Boone said quite matter-of-factly to Clara, "You must return to the practice room and ask that troubled spirit what she wants. Come. I will go with you." And she took Clara's hand.

Reassured by her teacher's words and by her presence, Clara did go back upstairs. From the door of the music room, she saw the figure quite distinctly, but Miss Boone later reported having only a hazy view of the child.

"Go ahead—ask her," Miss Boone prompted Clara.

Clara asked, "What in the name of the Lord do you want?" Somewhere (from a nurse? from an elderly aunt?) she had learned the traditional way of addressing spirits.

In response to Clara's question, the small ghost identified herself as Lizzie Davis, daughter of the Colonel Davis who had built the fine old house then occupied by the Brinkley Female College. Then she reportedly said, "Valuables are buried in a jar under a stump fifty yards from the house." She pointed a scrawny finger in the direction of the stump. Then she disappeared.

Clara heard the message quite distinctly, and so did another student who was in the room, but Miss Boone said she was not able to distinguish the words.

The return of the ghost and the message about the buried treasure created great excitement in the school. And with fifty flurried females reporting the strange events, much of Memphis shared the agitation occasioned by the visitations.

The excitement intensified when Clara's father announced that he intended to help his daughter dig for the buried jar.

A large crowd of spectators gathered in the yard to watch the digging, and there was considerable pushing and shoving as they all tried to get near enough to see what Clara, her father, and a helper he had brought along were doing.

First Mr. Robertson stepped off the specified fifty feet from the corner of the house and selected the proper stump. Then Clara began digging. The heavy shovel was difficult for her to handle, and the ground was hard.

From excitement or exertion, it was hard to tell which, Clara fainted dead away. The search had to be halted until she was revived. After she regained consciousness, somebody brought a chair from a classroom, and Clara sat near the stump.

After things calmed down, Mr. Robertson handed the shovel to his helper, and that man began to excavate a sizable hole around the stump.

"Careful now. Careful." Mr. Robertson warned. The hole was getting deeper and deeper.

"Better summon that little ghost girl to come dig. Call little Lizzie!" someone in the crowd called. There was much laughter.

Just then the shovel struck a hard object.

Mr. Robertson got down into the hole and lifted out a large glass jar, the kind frequently found in drug stores of the period. The jar had a sticky coating of mold and mud, but spectators saw a faded brown envelope and several small packages inside.

"Open it! Open it! Open it!" the crowd chanted.

But Mr. Robertson shook his head. The ghost, he explained, had said that the jar was not to be opened for sixty days.

Mr. Robertson was as curious about the contents of the jar and as eager to open it as any of the spectators were—likely more so—but, as he told the watchers, he believed he had better do exactly what the pitiful little phantom had said to do.

"She—the ghost—told Clara not to open the jar for sixty days, so we will wait," he said. He wrapped the jar in heavy paper and took it home with him.

News of the discovery of the mystery jar swept through Memphis. Accounts of the eerie doings filled columns of the local newspaper (*The Memphis Avalanche*), and people talked of little else.

Women were afraid to be left alone after dark, and even brave men avoided walking alone down Memphis' poorly lighted streets. Children had terrible nightmares about bony ghosts in pink garments. Bartenders did a thriving business selling a potent concoction called "Ghost Cocktails."

From as far away as Bolivar, Tennessee, and Holly Springs, Mississippi, came reports of sightings of the pink-clad wraith.

Meantime, Mr. Robertson was faced with the problem

87

of protecting the precious jar until the late April date when it could be opened. The safest place, it seems, would have been in the vault of the bank, but the ghostly instructions reportedly contained a clause requiring that the jar be kept on the Robertsons' premises.

The jar, Mr. Robertson knew, would be a tempting prize for burglars as well as for curiosity-seekers, so it was of the utmost importance that it be hidden in a place so obscure or so unlikely that no one would think of looking for it there. He considered and discarded the advisability of hiding the jar inside a chimney, covering it with flour in the barrel in the pantry, storing it in a trunk of old clothes in the attic, lowering it into the cistern, or concealing it behind a false wall in a closet.

After he had cudgeled his brain as hard as he could and was about to despair of thinking of a safe depository for the jar, Mr. Robertson suddenly had a brilliant idea.

The Robertsons had, to the rear of their home, a sturdy privy. It was a three-holer, discreetly and artfully screened by a trellis of climbing roses and honeysuckle.

This outhouse became the hiding place for the glass jar. Mr. Robertson tied a stout cord around the neck of the container and suspended it out of sight beneath a seat. He told no one about its location, not even Clara.

By the time April arrived, Memphis was mad with speculation about the contents of the jar. Interest was so great that Mr. Robertson arranged to open the jar on the stage of the Greenlaw Opera House on Second Street in full view of everyone in attendance. He rented the opera house for the occasion, already referred to in Memphis as "the grand opening."

The ghostly visitor had lusterless, sunken eyes, her form was emaciated, and her musty, moldy pink dress smelled of the grave.

88

Then an upsetting accident occurred.

A few nights before the date set for the jar's opening, a group of friends were visiting Mr. Robertson at his home. They were conversing in the parlor when they heard unusual noises in the back yard.

Mr. Robertson went out to investigate.

He stayed outside so long that his friends became concerned. Their concern changed to alarm when a servant dashed into the parlor and shouted, "Mr. Robertson—he laying out there with blood everywhere—must be dead!"

The friends rushed out into the yard where they did indeed find Mr. Robertson lying in a pool of blood. However, he was not dead, only unconscious as a result of a blow on his head.

A doctor, Dr. II. J. Shaw, was summoned. Dr. Shaw revived Mr. Robertson and treated a jagged four-inch wound on his head.

When he was able to speak, Mr. Robertson told of being confronted by four burly men who grabbed him and threatened him with instant death unless he showed them where the jar was hidden. Thoroughly frightened, Mr. Robertson showed them the secret hiding place. After the ruffians had the jar in their possession, one of them struck Mr. Robertson a vicious blow on the head with a metal intrument, rendering him insensible.

So the jar was gone. No trace was ever found of the jar or of the men who stole it.

The disappearance of the celebrated jar was marked by the appearance of skeptics who declared the whole thing was a fraud, a giant hoax. Such accusations upset Mr. Robertson, a man with a solid reputation for honesty and integrity, and he was eventually prodded into replying to the charges. He published affidavits from reputable men with personal knowledge of the entire series of events, and he himself verified the accuracy of the story from beginning to frustrating end. Signing the affidavits were Joseph L. Pierson, Ransom Christopher, Dr. H. J. Shaw, William Taylor, and Police Officer Patrick McElroy, all well known and respected residents of Memphis.

There was a final episode. Several days after the jar was stolen, Clara Robertson attended a seance to try to learn what the jar had contained. According to newspaper reports of the event, Clara went into a trance. In this state, she communed with the spirit of Lizzie Davis who told her that the jar had held $2,000 in gold coins, a diamond necklace, a set of gold jewelry, and an envelope of "valuable papers." The treasure had presumably been buried during The War to protect it from Yankee seizure.

The identity of one of the thieves was also revealed during the seance, the report said, but he was never apprehended.

Memphis gradually returned to normal, and the interests of its citizens turned to other things. Occasionally something would happen to remind them of the great jar mystery, and they would speculate about the whole strange series of happenings again.

Such a reminder occurred in 1876 when eighteen-year-old Clara Robertson married a wealthy seventy-two-year-old man. They went to Philadelphia to the Centennial Exposition on their honeymoon, and they reportedly settled in Vanndale, Arkansas, where they reared several children.

In later years, Clara was described as a pleasant, jolly woman who liked to entertain listeners with stories of the spirit of Lizzie Davis and of the mysterious glass jar. She also told of having in her possession letters from President U. S. Grant and Queen Victoria expressing interest in the girl ghost and the jar.

The building that had housed the Brinkley Female Col-

lege stood in Memphis until it was demolished and moved to Jonesboro, Arkansas, in the summer of 1972 by Jim Williams, a Memphis businessman.

In its last years, the house had become a shabby, rundown tenement, cut up into small apartments and cheap rental rooms. Yet, despite its peeling paint and rotting timbers, despite the rubbish scattered in what had once been formal gardens, it retained indelible marks of dignity and beauty. The six tall columns across the front porch, the upstairs balcony above the wide entryway, the graceful cupola on the sloping roof proclaimed it as a building that had once "really been something."

The mansion had been built by a Colonel Davis (also spelled in old records Davie and Davidson) who apparently sold it after the death of his beloved little daughter, Lizzie.

Lizzie was buried in Winchester Cemetery, a site now converted into a public park and playground. Land for the city cemetery was donated by Memphis' first mayor, Marcus B. Winchester, about 1828.

In 1931, when the cemetery was made into a park, information on all the tombstones was recorded before the graves were moved. These cemetery records, filed in the Memphis collection at the public library, include in their listings, "Davis Child—Daughter of J. D. Davis—Died October 6, 1863."

The official records don't say so, but there is a handed-down story in Memphis that the Davis child was buried in a pink dress because it was her very favorite dress. The front of that little pink dress, they say, was stained by the juice of ripe strawberries which the child had spilled on it the day she died.

In its last years, the house had become a shabby, rundown tenement, cut up into small apartments and cheap rental rooms.

During the Battle of Shiloh, Cherry Mansion in Savannah, Tennessee, was used as Federal headquarters. General Grant was in command.

Shiloh Revisited

Terry Smith is a history buff. Confederate history is his major interest, and the Battle of Shiloh is his specialty. Terry lives in Savannah, Tennessee, about ten miles across the Tennessee River from that historic battlefield.

For almost as long as he can remember, Terry has hiked back and forth across the battlefield, tracing the placements of the Confederate and the Federal troops and following the lines of battle. The Peach Orchard, Hell's Hollow, Bloody Pond, Hornet's Nest—Terry knows them all. He has stood beneath the oak where Confederate General Albert Sidney Johnston died of a leg wound, a wound that needed only a simple tourniquet to staunch the fatal loss of blood. He knows the spot where United States General W. H. L. Wallace lay mortally wounded during the stormy night that followed the first day's engagement.

He has walked through the National Cemetery above the river, among the precise rows of white stones that mark the burial places of more than 3,000 Union dead, and, a few miles away, he has stood beside the burial trenches where the bodies of Confederate soldiers were stacked seven deep.

Terry Smith knows the stories of Shiloh, the history and the legends, and he shares his knowledge of the place with visitors who want to listen.

There are other stories that Terry is more selective about sharing, stories dealing with his encounters with the ghosts of Shiloh.

If ever a battlefield should have ghosts, it is Shiloh. Yet National Park officials there say, "No, there are no ghosts here. We have no record of any stories about ghosts at Shiloh."

No ghostly tales about the gallant Drummer Boy of Shiloh? Surely on still nights the rhythms of the lad's drum must echo along the Sunken Road at Shiloh. But, "No," the authorities say, "not even the ghost of the Drummer Boy haunts Shiloh."

Terry Smith knows that the battlefield should have several ghosts, certainly including the fabled Drummer Boy, but even he says he has had no ghostly encounters there.

He has, however, had two strange experiences which he feels certain are connected with the conflict at Shiloh. Each of these experiences occurred at Cherry Mansion in Savannah, headquarters for Federal officers before, during, and after the Battle of Shiloh.

This fine old house with its wide front porch, its bannistered second-story balcony, and its tall outside chimneys was built about 1830. It overlooks the Tennessee River and stands on the spot where James Rudd, who ran a ferry on the river, built a rough log cabin in 1815.

David Robinson bought the site from Rudd, removed the cabin and built a comfortable house there. The house became a wedding gift to his daughter when she married W.

H. Cherry.

The new owners enlarged and beautified the property, adding, among other improvements, a low stone wall to encircle the house and gardens. The wall remains today as do other distinctive features of Cherry Mansion: the eighteen-inch-thick walls of the house, the wide fan-lighted doorway, the heart pine flooring, the handcrafted cabinets and book-cases, and the Southern plantings of evergreens and flowering shrubs.

Mr. Cherry combined his plantation interests with investments in river transportation (shipping cotton to the Memphis market could be quite profitable) to become a very wealthy man.

He was also a Union sympathizer.

Many of his neighbors shared his loyalty to the Union cause, and Savannah, there in southwestern Tennessee, became a Yankee stronghold.

Troops from Illinois and Ohio found a friendly welcome when they arrived in Savannah in March of 1862. At the invitation of Mr. Cherry, the officers established their head-quarters in his fine home, the first of many Yankee officers to be quartered there.

Terry Smith lives across the street from Cherry Mansion, and he knows the place and its owners, Mr. and Mrs. Robert B. Guinn, Jr., well.

During the summer of 1976, Terry Smith and several other students were employed at Shiloh National Military Park. Terry was a member of a gun crew that fired an authentic Yankee cannon several times daily for the entertainment and education of tourists.

The youths were dressed in Union artillery uniforms (some wags called them Union suits—and members of the firing team were too young to understand the joke), wool garments mighty hot for wearing during a Tennessee summer.

In the summer of 1976, Terry Smith and several other students fired an authentic Yankee cannon for the tourists visiting Shiloh Military Park.

Another member of the demonstration gunnery squad was John Frank, referred to by his fellow artillerymen as their "token Yankee." Most of the summer employees of the park lived in nearby Tennessee and Mississippi towns.

One night in late June, 1976, Terry Smith and John Frank were sitting on the front porch of Cherry Mansion with Mary Ann Guinn, daughter of the owners of the home. It was a little after 11:00 p.m., and the three young people were talking softly so as not to disturb Mary Ann's parents.

Their conversation was interrupted by the sound of footsteps approaching the house. They looked across the driveway and the wall, and they saw a gentleman walking down the street toward the house. He was wearing a loose-fitting white suit, possibly linen, and he had gray hair and a full gray beard. His carriage was erect, and he walked with the purposeful stride of a man with a definite goal in mind. He was not out for a leisurely stroll.

"Who is that?" Terry whispered.

Mary Ann shook her head. "I never saw him before," she replied. "He doesn't look as if he belongs here."

John Frank, being only a token Yankee instead of a native, was not expected to know the walker.

The stranger walked up to the metal historical marker, the one that gives a brief history of Cherry Mansion, and stood there reading the inscription. He did not hurry with his reading: it was almost as if he were checking the text for accuracy.

Then he vanished. Completely. While Mary Ann, Terry, and John looked right at him, he disappeared. There was no sound of footsteps, no glimpse of a retreating figure.

The mystified—and somewhat shaken—trio hurried from the porch and into the street where they had last seen the man standing. The street was deserted. Nobody—nothing—was stirring.

The marker reads:

CHERRY MANSION
4C 22

A house built here by James Rudd, pioneer ferry operator, was replaced by a house built by David Robinson, whose son-in-law, William H. Cherry, improved and enlarged it. Maj. Gen. C.F. Smith, Federal army commander, had headquarters here, where he died and was succeeded by Maj. Gen. U.S. Grant. Maj. Gen. Don Carlos Buell, commanding Federal Army of the Ohio, also used it for a short while. Maj. Gen. W.H.L. Wallace, mortally wounded at Shiloh, died here.

The stranger walked up to the metal historical marker and read the inscription of the brief history of Cherry Mansion.

The three of them made a quick but methodical search of the neighborhood, just to satisfy themselves absolutely that no human being was about. They found nothing.

Later, when they told of the experience, listeners shook their heads. "Strange," they said. "Mighty strange." No one doubted the truth of the story, but no one had an explanation for it either.

Several people who heard descriptions of the nocturnal visitor remarked that the white suit he wore resembled the linen suits prosperous planters wore back before The War. They added that the man's hair style and his beard seemed to fit the period, too.

They wondered, a few of them, if Cherry's ghost, the ghost of the wealthy planter, might have paid a visit to his mansion.

Terry wondered, too.

An earlier encounter with a strange visitor at Cherry Mansion was even more puzzling and frightening for Terry.

The youth had often heard the Guinns' long-time servant tell of unusual happenings in the house, peculiar noises and such. She told of hearing often the sound of heavy footsteps hurrying across the front porch, yet when she went to the door, no one was ever there. It happened again and again, she said.

"Sounds like the man is wearing big boots. And sounds like he's in a powerful hurry to get to the door with an important message for somebody. Who it is or what he wants, I don't know. But he keeps coming," the servant said.

Terry was interested in the woman's story, but he was not frightened by it. The Guinns tended to discount the story completely.

Perhaps Terry was thinking of the story of the footsteps when he walked toward the porch of the empty house one night in 1975. The Guinn family had gone out of town for a few days, and Terry, their neighbor, had agreed to feed their animals and check on the house while they were away.

The peacocks had already gone to roost when Terry began his rounds (he was later than he had intended to be), but he saw that the birds had food and water for the next day. He also fed and watered the animals, and he was walking across the lawn toward his home when he decided he had better make certain that the big front door of Cherry Mansion was securely locked. He turned around and walked toward the front porch.

For some reason, Terry's attention was attracted to the dormer window, high in the attic above the porch. A man stood at that window peering down at Terry.

The intruder was bearded, and he was wearing a dark, wide-brimmed hat, the kind worn by officers during the Civil War. The figure gazed hard at Terry. Terry returned the gaze, looking hard at the bearded face. Then he whirled and ran for home.

"I was scared," Terry admits. "That face in the window wasn't like anything I've ever seen before—or since. I saw the man as plain as I've ever seen anything, and I'll never forget how he looked at me. Never."

Terry is sure—as sure as it is possible to be—that he had an encounter with the ghost of a Union officer who had strong ties with Cherry Mansion. But who? General U. S. Grant? General W. H. L. Wallace? General C. F. Smith? Each of them had reason to haunt Cherry Mansion.

General Grant had taken up residence at Cherry Mansion in March, 1862, arriving by boat from Fort Henry, about one hundred miles away. His orders were to prepare the Yankee troops assembling at and near Pittsburg Landing for a decisive battle with Rebel forces. The battle, they thought, would be fought at Corinth, Mississippi.

The Rebel forces had other plans. Their strategy was to

Perhaps it was the ghost of General W. H. L. Wallace whom Terry Smith saw looking down at him from an upstairs window.

104

stage a surprise attack on the Union forces before those forces were strengthened by the expected arrival of reinforcements under the command of General San Carlos Buell.

The Rebel strategy almost succeeded.

General Grant was having breakfast at Cherry Mansion that April Sunday when he heard the distant rumbling of cannon.

"Gentlemen," he said to his staff members, "the ball is in motion. Let us be off." He put his coffee cup down and hobbled from the room.

The Union commander had injured his ankle two days earlier when his horse slipped on wet ground near Pittsburg Landing and fell on him. The soft ground prevented General Grant from suffering a more serious injury, but a severely sprained ankle made it necessary for him to use a crutch. The crutch went with him as he boarded the boat bound for Pittsburg Landing, and it was strapped to his saddle as he rode up the bluff to take command at the Battle of Shiloh.

The ache of the ankle and the memories of the death-drenched battlefield kept General Grant awake a long, long time that night.

Was it the ghost of General Grant looking down at Terry Smith from the high window at Cherry Mansion?

Or was it General C. L. Smith's apparition he saw?

General Smith had been one of the early Union arrivals in Savannah. It was he who established headquarters at Cherry Mansion (he was described as an experienced officer who never neglected the creature comforts), and he was present to greet other officers when they arrived. Together they plotted the strategy which they believed would crush the Confederacy.

In late March, several days before the Battle of Shiloh, General Smith was ordered to bed because of an infected leg. He had skinned his shin on the seat of a rowboat, and the

105

injury failed to heal. So that April morning when other officers hurried off to Shiloh, General Smith lay in bed at Cherry Mansion, listening to the distant guns and cursing the fate that made him miss the battle.

General Smith died in late April there at Cherry Mansion. Cause of death was listed as blood poisoning, but military men who knew him best did not agree. His death, they said, was hastened by outrage, frustration, and heartbreak over a senseless injury that kept him away from the action at Shiloh.

Could it have been the ghost of General Smith, watching from the high window for a courier from Shiloh, whom Terry saw?

Or could it have been the ghost of General W. H. L. Wallace?

General Wallace was a mid-western lawyer who had seen action in the Mexican War. General Grant depended heavily on General Wallace's experience and stability, so General Wallace was in Savannah to take command of key units in the expected battle.

As that battle neared, Mrs. Wallace had a premonition, a sort of dream, that her husband was going to be killed. The vision was so vivid that she could not erase it from her thoughts. She left her home and booked passage on a steamboat bound for Savannah.

Mrs. Wallace arrived in Savannah only a few hours after the fighting at Shiloh began. Her husband, she learned, was on the battlefront. So, as wives of soldiers have done for thousands of years, Mrs. Wallace sat and waited for the dreaded news she knew would come.

When the messenger arrived at Cherry Mansion, hurrying across the porch in his heavy boots, she tried to concentrate on his words: "General Wallace...bravery under fire...Hornet's Nest...rallying his men...terrible loss of life...body not yet recovered...." She tried to listen to the words, but all she could hear was her heart pounding, "He's dead. He's dead. He's dead."

During the night, a violent thunderstorm broke over the battlefield.

At daylight next day, burial squads moved into the field to pick up the dead. Among the bodies at the Hornet's Nest, where so many brave men died, they found General Wallace, shot through the head but alive.

The general was taken by boat to Cherry Mansion. Despite his wound, he recognized his wife, and they had a tender reunion.

The wound, however, was mortal. For four days, General Wallace lingered, occasionally conscious, more often drifting off into deep sleep. During those four days, Mrs. Wallace sat beside her husband's bed with her hand in his. Though he could not see, General Wallace during his conscious moments ran his fingers over the wedding ring he had given his wife. The touch of the ring seemed to give him reassurance and comfort.

His final words, there in the parlor of Cherry Mansion, were, "We shall meet in heaven."

So perhaps it was the ghost of General Wallace whom Terry saw.

Grant? Smith? Wallace? Someone else? Terry does not know. He only knows that he saw in that dormer window the face of a troubled man, a man who he feels was a part of that tragic conflict called Shiloh.

The old Eakin house at 610 North Jefferson Street in Shelby-ville does not look the same with its upper story missing.

The Exorcism of Aunt Crecy

For almost forty years a gentle ghost haunted the old Eakin home at 610 North Jefferson Street in Shelbyville. People who lived in the house called the spirit Aunt Crecy, though she was not really kin to them. Her real name was Lucretia Pearson Eakin, wife of John Eakin, and she had lived in that house for half a century before her death in the early 1890s.

Lucretia Pearson grew up in the Flatcreek community near Shelbyville. Her family traded in Shelbyville, making the seven-mile trip by wagon, and it was there that she met a prosperous Irish merchant named John Eakin.

Courtship followed that meeting. As Lucretia (her family and friends called her Crecy) talked shyly of becoming Mrs. Eakin, her friends teased, "Will you be Mrs. John Eakin or Mrs. Spencer Eakin? Mrs. Alexander Eakin or Mrs. William Eakin? Or, perhaps, will you be Mrs. Thomas Eakin? Which one of those fine Irish lads will you wed? Can you tell them apart, Crecy?"

And though Crecy blushingly replied that it was John Eakin she intended to marry, as they all knew, she did understand how there could be some confusion with so many young men in the Eakin family.

John—Crecy's intended—had come to Shelbyville from Ireland in 1817. Three years later, his brother, Spencer, joined him. The brothers became business partners, were so successful, and wrote letters containing such enthusiastic accounts of opportunities in the area that in 1822 the entire Eakin family (with the exception of one married sister) crossed the Atlantic and made their way to Shelbyville.

Having chosen his bride, John built a tall, sturdy, red brick house out on Fairfield Pike, the first of five such substantial dwellings built by the Eakin family. The property is now a part of Shelbyville, but at the time it was built, it was "out in the country."

Mrs. Eakin was proud of her fine house, but she did wish that her husband had built it in town. Having grown up in the country, she had always looked forward to living in town where she could have close neighbors, could be in walking distance of stores and shops, and could be near the church.

Being near the church was what she wanted most of all. She was a devout Presbyterian, and it troubled her that the distance from her home to the Shelbyville Presbyterian Church kept her from being as faithful in attendance as she wanted to be. She seldom missed Sunday worship, but it was not always convenient or even possible for her to attend mid-week prayer services and meetings of the women's missionary groups, or to be active in other work of the church.

So Mrs. Eakin—Crecy—began a gentle campaign to persuade her husband to move to town. She was a good, loving, obedient wife, not given to nagging, but she used every possible opportunity to call her husband's attention to the desirability of establishing residency in downtown Shelbyville.

In her campaign, she leaned heavily on her wish to be near the Presbyterian Church. While her husband might readily dismiss her desire for close neighbors ("Women waste time gossiping") or her wish to be near stores and shops ("Just tell me what you need, and I'll bring it to you"), he could not fail to be impressed by her desire to be more deeply involved in the work of the church.

Her campaign was not immediately successful (Crecy had not expected it to be—she was a patient woman), but as time went by, John Eakin fell under the influence of her gentle persuasion. Finally, following an occasion when Crecy had been deeply disappointed over not being able to attend a missionary rally at the Presbyterian Church, John surrendered. He loved his wife, and he did want her to be happy.

"All right," he said. "If you really want to move to town, we will. I'll build you a house in the shadow of the steeple of the Presbyterian Church!"

And he did.

The house, located across the street from the church, was built of brick, and it was two stories tall. There was a graceful cupola on the roof, and the kitchen and dining room were in the basement. Windows on the first and second floors opened onto identical balconies. It was completed in 1835, and John and Crecy Eakin moved to town.

"Oh, John," Crecy exclaimed as she walked through the rooms of her new house, "isn't it beautiful! So lovely! I will never, never leave it. Never!"

And so Crecy Eakin became a part of the life of Shelbyville. She, of course, became a veritable pillar in the Presbyterian Church, working in all departments and supporting all its worthy causes.

Other activities in town claimed her attention, also. She

made new friends among the ladies and joined them for sewing circles, for musicales, and for teas ("Really, John, we don't spend all our time gossiping!"). She enjoyed going with her husband to parties and banquets at the rambling Holland House, the inn so closely bound to the early history of Shelbyville.

She had heard the story of the fabulous banquet at Holland House honoring Andrew Jackson (that, however, was before she moved to town), and she knew of the visits there of John Murrell, the outlaw.

Her husband had told her of the time Murrell came to Shelbyville posing as a noted preacher ("He didn't say he was Presbyterian, did he?"..."No, I don't think so.") and how he ran off with all the money in the collection plates, quite a sizable amount. Murrell's sermon had been long and impassioned, John Eakin reported, providing ample time for his henchmen to steal the horses which worshippers had tied in the grove near the church.

Crecy, in turn, told John stories she had heard about the Murrell gang and their rendezvous at nearby Farmington.

"I've seen the house where the gang used to meet. They say it's haunted," Crecy said. "They say the ghost of one of Murrell's gang is there. They had a fight in that house one night—quarreling over some money they had stolen—and a man was killed. They say his blood stains are still on the wall[*] and nobody can scrub them off."

John, being Irish, did not discount the story of the ghost.

[*]*A later occupant of the house, Mrs. W. C. Ransom, dealt with the ghost legend by the simple act of covering the bloodstains with wallpaper, thus silencing a great deal of talk and speculation. The house burned during a thunderstorm in 1968.*

Ruins of the house at Farmington haunted by one of the Murrell gang.

113

Always, when they talked of Holland House, Crecy would add contentedly, "Not even Holland House is as nice as my house."

As Crecy grew older, she seemed to love her house more. While she was not what could be called an immaculate housekeeper, the whole house reflected the care and attention she lavished on it. And when guests exclaimed, "What a charming house!" she smiled in agreement.

Though she found pleasure in the entire house, her favorite room was her upstairs sitting room. In her later life, this room became her retreat, a haven where she could sort out her memories and commune with her soul.

She continued to attend church services as long as she was physically able, long after she was forced to curtail other activities. On pleasant days, she sat in a rocking chair in the yard, greeting friends who passed by and hearing from them the news of the town. By then, nearly everybody called her Aunt Crecy.

Lucretia Pearson Eakin died in the early 1890s, leaving the house she loved.

But did she, in death, really leave the house?

Some residents of Shelbyville say she did not, that she loved the house too much to leave it and that, for years, her spirit lingered in those familiar rooms.

After Mrs. Eakin's death, the property was sold to Ernest Coldwell, a lawyer, who moved his family there. Mr. and Mrs. Coldwell's daughter, Amy, was born in the house and lived there until she was a young lady.

Amy, now Mrs. Sydney D. McGrew of Shelbyville, recalls that members of her family were always aware of the presence of Mrs. Eakin's ghost in the house.

"It was a friendly, protective presence, and we were never frightened by it," she says.

There were no startling, dramatic manifestations of the

114

ghost's presence, only gentle reminders of a caring spirit: open windows would be closed by unseen hands during sudden summer showers or furniture might be moved ever so slightly or flowers rearranged in a vase or pictures straightened on a wall.

"Amy, run upstairs and pull the windows down—I know it's raining in!" her mother might say. And Amy would call from upstairs, "Mama! The windows are already down!"

"I guess Aunt Crecy beat you to it." Aunt Crecy was credited for many such thoughtful deeds.

It was in the upstairs sitting room that Aunt Crecy's presence was most often felt. The swaying of a rocker, the rustle of pages of a book, the rearrangements of items on a table—small reminders of a caring presence.

Mrs. McGrew recalls the day when she was about twelve and had carelessly left her bicycle leaning against the double doors that opened onto a side porch. Her mother had cautioned her often about leaving the bike there, pointing out that it would be knocked over by anyone entering the door.

The little girl remembered her mother's warning and was walking toward the doors to move her bicycle when one of the doors opened, the bicycle was pushed out of the way, and the door closed.

Nobody was there.

Amy, who was not afraid, knew that Aunt Crecy was taking care of her, reminding her to be more thoughtful.

Years passed. Amy married and moved from the house. As her parents grew older, they took an apartment at The Dixie Hotel (long famous for its fine food and as a gathering place for horse fanciers) during the winter, returning to their home for brief periods of time.

It was during such a visit in 1931 that fire broke out in the old Eakin house.

Mrs. Coldwell had invited some friends to meet her at

Aunt Crecy's thoughtfulness continued after her death, and often the windows were closed by her caring spirit before the rains could spoil the carpet.

the house for an afternoon of bridge, and they were playing cards downstairs. Mr. Coldwell was in the kitchen supervising the cooking of a 'possum. 'Possum was not included on the menu at The Dixie Hotel, and one of his friends had supplied this treat for him.

The bridge players were engrossed in their game, and Mr. Coldwell was totally involved in getting the 'possum cooked properly. They all heard the town's fire alarm, but nobody really paid any attention to it until firemen burst into the house.

"Your house is on fire!" they shouted. "What do you want us to save?"

Mr. Coldwell directed, first of all, that the hot stove and the 'possum be carried to safety. As soon as this was taken care of, Mr. Coldwell, against the orders of the firemen, then went upstairs and retrieved his favorite fishing rod.

By that time, the blaze was under control. It had apparently started from defective wiring on the second floor, and it was in that part of the house that the greatest damage was done. The upstairs sitting room, Aunt Crecy's room, was gutted by the flames. In fact, the entire top floor was so badly damaged that it had to be torn away. The lower floor had only smoke and water damage.

The old house is lovely again now, but, with its upper story missing, it does not look the way it used to when Lucretia Pearson Eakin lived there.

Her ghost has gone, too.

Her presence has not been felt in the house since that day in 1931 when fire destroyed her sitting room, her haven.

117

"The Wedding Cake" in Bolivar where Uncle Dave rocked so long that he expected to carry the habit into eternity.

The Restless Rocker

 Uncle Dave Parran rocked on the porch of his house in Bolivar for so many years and entertained so many listeners with his stories there that people just naturally expected to see him rocking and hear his cordial greeting every time they passed the house. Even after he died back in 1936—he was 86 then—they still half-expected to see him rocking on the porch, and they caught themselves about to wave or to speak to the old gentleman. It wasn't right for him to be gone: the porch was too still and too empty.

Nobody remembers now who first noticed or exactly when they noticed that Uncle Dave's chair was rocking back and forth on the porch, just the way it used to do. Nobody was in the chair, but it was rocking just the way it did when Uncle Dave sat there.

Before long, many passersby reported that on calm, windless days, when there was not even the fleeting suggestion of a breeze, Uncle Dave's chair moved rhythmically back and forth. People passing along Bills Street and seeing the empty chair rocking on the porch commented, "Uncle Dave is out porch-rocking and people-watching today." And nobody has ever been frightened by the phenomenon—it seems so completely natural.

People-watching was one of Uncle Dave's favorite activities. He liked people, genuinely liked them. He liked to observe them, speculate about their actions, talk to them, and listen to them. As the years passed, his talent for talking, for telling the tales of "I remember—" and his gift of listening, of hearing with his heart as well as with his ears, seasoned and mellowed.

For almost three quarters of a century, Uncle Dave Parran practiced his people-watching on the courthouse square at Bolivar, county seat of Hardeman County. He was an undertaker, and his place of business was on West Market Street, right on the square. When he wasn't busy (small-town undertakers generally had more leisure time than did clerks in general stores or farmers), he would sit out in front of his establishment and watch the comings and goings of the townspeople.

He didn't spend all his time just watching, of course. Many friends stopped to talk with him there on the sidewalk. While he leaned his chair back against the building, making himself comfortable, they discussed crops and politics and local happenings and news from Memphis. If the conversations lengthened, there were extra chairs inside the building that could be—and were—brought out to the sidewalk.

Though he didn't realize it, Uncle Dave was storing up local lore to be shared, years later, with generations of younger visitors, ones who came after he had swapped his straight chair on the sidewalk for a rocking chair on his porch.

Actually he didn't ever entirely give up his downtown

Passersby who see the chair swaying know that Uncle Dave is on the porch watching people, one of his favorite occupations for many years.

121

vantage point, but after he passed his eightieth birthday, he did spend more time at home than he did on the square. He never did completely retire from his undertaking business either, just eased off work a little.

By that time, by the time he was up in his eighties, nearly everybody in Bolivar called him Uncle Dave. The "uncle" was a prefix of affectionate respect, started by his nephew and nieces when he was a young man, echoed by their friends, and passed on to succeeding generations. Only his contemporaries called him David, and as the years sped by, not many of them remained.

The house where Uncle Dave rocked was called The Wedding Cake. He loved that house and liked to tell about it.

"Just look at the house and you can see that it looks like a wedding cake, all that frilly trimming around the eaves and the fancy bannisters here on the porch. It got its name when John Houston Bills built it as a wedding gift for his Lucy. Lucy was his daughter who married the newspaperman, Wilbur Armistead. Mr. Bills hired Fletcher Sloan to design the house, and maybe he tried to make it look like a decorated wedding cake since it was a wedding present.

"Don't you think it's a good name for this house?" he would ask. "The Wedding Cake. I like the name."

By the time Uncle Dave was spending most of his days on the porch of The Wedding Cake instead of downtown Bolivar, he had become a delightful source of local history. He was almost the only person left in Bolivar who could tell about the May night in 1864 when the Yankees burned the courthouse. It was not one of Uncle Dave's favorite stories, but he could describe how troops under the command of General Sturgis set fire to the courthouse, to the Baptist Church, to business places around the square. It was a searing scene of destruction (some Rebels dubbed it a cruel act of retaliation by General Sturgis after he was outmaneuvered

122

and outfought by Confederate General N. B. Forrest in an engagement between Bolivar and Corinth, Mississippi) that Uncle Dave, a youth of fourteen at the time, recalled in disquieting detail.

He could tell amusing tales about The War, too. There was the Sunday, he recalled, when the widow Coates came to church without wearing her bustle. The widow Coates was usually fashionably dressed (and bustles were in fashion), but it was a very hot Sunday, so she left off that item of apparel when she sallied forth to the Presbyterian Church that summer Sunday.

Right in the midst of morning prayer, word reached the church that the Yankees were on the outskirts of town.

The widow rose from her knees and hurried out of the church. As she left the sanctuary, she whispered something to one of her female friends about having to "get my bustle on before they get here." It seemed a bit strange, the confidant admitted later, that Mrs. Coates should want to rush home and get dressed up for the arrival of enemy troops.

Actually the widow Coates wasn't at all concerned with dressing up for the Yankees: she had $50,000 in currency sewed to the padding of her bustle, and she had no intention of letting Yankee soldiers find that unattended treasure. The money was not even hers: it had been entrusted to her for safekeeping by Colonel Ezekiel McNeal, so she was quite concerned about preventing its loss.

Mrs. Coates did get home just in time, despite dropping her house key on the sidewalk downtown and having to pause precious minutes to retrieve it, to let herself into her home, adjust her bustle, and catch her breath before Yankee soldiers came to search the premises.

After that experience, the widow wore her precious bustle winter and summer (even when the temperature played tag with 100 degrees) until the war ended and she

Priscilla McNeal's grave marker in Polk Cemetery.

returned the bills safely to Colonel McNeal.

Uncle Dave liked to tell that tale to listeners gathered around his rocking chair.

Then there was the story he told of little Georgia Wood whose father, Dr. George Wood, was away fighting in the Confederate Army.

A young Federal officer quartered in the Wood home (Bolivar was occupied by Federal forces from the spring of 1862 until the war ended) asked the little girl to come sit beside him on the sofa.

Georgia shook her head.

Thinking the child was timid, the officer coaxed, "Please come sit by me. I have a little girl about your size. I won't hurt you. Don't be afraid."

"I'm not afraid," Georgia retorted. "I can't sit down— our money is sewed in my hoops!"

The child was indeed burdened with a trove of silver coins so cumbersome that she could not sit down.

The Yankee officer, at risk to himself and his career, offered to keep the money safe if Mrs. Wood would entrust it to him. She did, and he kept his promise faithfully.

Uncle Dave could tell such stories as long as he had an interested audience. Between audiences, he sat and rocked and remembered.

From his front porch, Uncle Dave could look across the street and see the McNeal Place, surely the most handsome house in Bolivar.

Uncle Dave remembered how, when he was a little boy, he used to watch for Mrs. McNeal to come out of that big house and walk across the road to the Polk Cemetery. She visited the cemetery every day to take fresh flowers to her daugher's grave, and David (he was not Uncle Dave then), standing at a respectful distance, watched that daily pilgrimage and wondered at the mother's devotion.

125

He had heard his own mother tell the story of Priscilla McNeal's death many times, and each telling made David sad.

Priscilla McNeal, the story went, died of pneumonia on July 16, 1854, at the age of eighteen, shortly before she was to have been married. She was the only child of Mr. and Mrs. Ezekiel Polk McNeal, and Mrs. McNeal never ceased grieving over the death of her daughter.

Even the building of McNeal Place, the grand Southern manor house rising three stories to its square cupola, did not divert her, did not lessen her grief. She watched with slight interest as workmen trimmed the west veranda and the second-story balcony with delicate Spanish grillwork depicting the four seasons, and she tried to share her husband's pride in the hand-carved mantles of Carrara marble. She helped supervise the planting of native shrubs and trees in the thirty-acre park around the house, and she did find solace in the rose gardens, the herb beds, the greenhouse.

But she kept thinking, "If only Priscilla could be here to enjoy this house, to walk in the gardens, to gather the flowers. If only Priscilla were here!" And every day she took fresh flowers to Priscilla's grave.

During the Federal occupation of Bolivar, the picket line was set up along the road bordering McNeal Place, blocking Mrs. McNeal's path to the cemetery. When soldiers, obeying orders, refused to let her cross the line to take flowers to Priscilla's grave, she appealed to the commanding officer who granted her a pass.

"Mrs. McNeal's pass, properly framed, hangs on the wall of McNeal Place," Uncle Dave would relate. He knew the story well.

He knew other stories about the Polk Cemetery, and he told many visitors about the epitaph Colonel Ezekiel Polk wrote for himself in the seventy-fourth year of his life. Incidentally, Uncle Dave added, Colonel Polk was referred to

126

Grave of Colonel Ezekiel Polk in the Polk Cemetery, Bolivar, Tennessee.

by some people as "the best buried man in Bolivar." He was buried three times: first (1824) in Old Hatchie Town, then at a site near the county jail in Bolivar, and finally (1846) in the Polk Cemetery.

Colonel Polk's unorthodox epitaph became an issue in the presidential campaign of his grandson, James Knox Polk. The candidate's opponents gave wide publicity to the lines of the epitaph reading,

Church and state will join their power,
And misery on the country show'r,
And Methodists with their camp bawling
Will be the cause of this down falling.

First fruits and tenths are odious things,
So are bishops, priests and kings.

127

Uncle Dave was quite familiar with that epitaph, but he paused to read it again nearly every time he visited the cemetery. Sometimes he pointed out the cracks in the stone where family members are reported to have chiseled out the offensive line about the "bawling" Methodists.

Polk was elected to the presidency despite his grandfather's irreligious poetry—and citizens of Bolivar staged a riotous celebration of his victory.

He knew hundreds of stories, Uncle Dave did, and he told them well.

In addition to being a people-watcher and a story-teller, Uncle Dave was a saver and a keeper. He liked to collect programs, newspaper clippings, photographs, invitations, announcements and such, particularly if they included the names of members of his family. He had a large family connection, and a collection of memorabilia to match.

He always meant to organize his keepsakes properly in files or scrapbooks or such, but he never quite got around to that. However, given time, he could nearly always locate a picture or a clipping or verify a date or a name when somebody needed such information.

As he grew older, his searches sometimes took place late at night or in the still hours before dawn. Occupants of The Wedding Cake grew accustomed to being roused from sleep by the sounds of drawers being opened and papers being shuffled, of light footsteps moving about the house.

"What's Uncle Dave looking for now?" they would ask themselves drowsily before sleep claimed them again.

Strangely enough, those same noises, the muffled sounds of an old man walking about in familiar and beloved rooms, are still heard in that house. Hearers are neither frightened nor particularly surprised: they are accustomed to Uncle Dave's ghostly roaming through rooms in search of things he saved and kept a long time ago.

Other story-tellers relate Uncle Dave's tales now, passing along bits of lore they learned from Bolivar's people-watcher.

But though Uncle Dave's voice is silent, his chair, his restless rocker, still sways gently on the porch at The Wedding Cake in Bolivar.

James Austin, pastor of the First Baptist Church in Rogers-ville, was reared by his grandparents. His grandfather left James his gold Elgin watch, which James shows to his son, Jay.

The Blessing

"You're not afraid of ghosts, are you?" the Reverend James L. Austin asked his bride.

"There might be ghosts—now I'm not saying there are, just that there might be—at the country pastorium where we're going to live. But you're not going to be afraid, are you?"

Mrs. James L. Austin (it still seemed strange to be called Mrs. Austin instead of Miss Lipscomb) knew her husband was teasing her. She laughed and teased back, "If you're not afraid, I won't be! You've been living out there all by yourself, and nothing has ever bothered you.

"And anyhow, I know you will protect me from any ghosts that might be lurking around," she said.

Though James Austin was teasing his bride, he did have some basis for his remarks. Ever since he had moved into the rural pastorium, located some three miles from Kingston, Tennessee, he had heard rumors of ghost tales connected with the place.

He had never had any frightening or unusual experiences in the house, but he could understand why it might have ghost stories associated with it. Very near the pastorium, right outside the bedroom window, were several graves. Buried there were the members of a family, all of whom had died of a strange and undiagnosed ailment. Perhaps they were victims of typhoid or of yellow fever, feared killers of the time. Neighbors used to say they were killed by drinking "poisoned water."

So James reminded his bride about those graves and teased her about ghosts at her new home.

It was late January, 1965, and the couple were in New York on their honeymoon. Kingston, Tennessee, seemed very far away.

Though she knew he was teasing about the possibility of ghosts at the pastorium, the bride also knew that her husband had been involved in supernatural experiences when he was growing up, before the two of them had met.

James was in his early 'teens, according to the story, when he had an eerie encounter with a luminous horse. He was living with his grandparents, Mr. and Mrs. James A. Austin, on their farm in the Taylor's Community, about seven miles from Cleveland, Tennessee, when it happened.

It was summertime, and there was a revival meeting in progress at the church in town. James, even then, had felt a strong call to the ministry, so it was natural that he would want to attend the revival services.

There was also a very attractive girl in town who attended the same church and who was pleased to have James escort her to the nightly services. She may have influenced James' faithful attendance at the revival.

James didn't have a car, and he was too young to drive if he had had one, so he rode his bicycle into town each night. He would leave his bicycle at the girl's house, and they would walk to church together.

After services, they would walk back to her house. Maybe James would stay a little while, talking to her on the porch and making polite conversation with her family. Sometimes they had refreshments, lemonade with oatmeal cookies or pound cake or maybe a cold watermelon or such.

Then James would get on his bicycle and ride back out to the farm. It was a lonely ride, but James rather enjoyed it. Nearly every night at church someone would ask, "Aren't you scared to ride so far by yourself at night?" James would laugh and shake his head. He wasn't scary, and he couldn't think of anybody or anything that might harm him.

On this particular night, James was riding home thinking all kinds of nice thoughts about the sermon and the minister and the music and the people who had been at church. Nice thoughts about his girl kept cropping up, too. He could have been thinking about her more than he was thinking about the revival services. It had been a very pleasant night.

He was getting pretty close to home when he glanced over and saw something white moving around in the field ahead of him.

"Wonder whose big white billy goat that is?" James thought, but even before he finished the thought, he saw that the white thing was too big to be a goat. It must be a cow, he decided, but by that time, he saw that the thing wasn't a white cow either.

It was a horse, a large white horse that glowed in the dark.

The animal was more magnificent than any horse James had ever seen, but the boy had no desire to stop and admire the horse's unusual beauty and grace. There was something foreboding about the creature, something frightening.

As he came opposite the horse, James was thankful for the strong fence that separated the field from the road: no

horse could jump over or break through that fence.

But as James watched, the glowing horse moved right through the strands of barbed wire, right through the fence, as though it were not there.

James pedaled his bike faster than he had ever pedaled before. When he reached the top of the hill, he took a quick look back over his shoulder. The horse was still there, standing beside the road and casting a brilliant glow into the darkness.

Again James pedaled as fast as he could. He wondered if the phantom horse was following him (do ghost horses make noise when they run?), but he was afraid to look back. He did not slow down or look behind him until he reached the familiar safety of his grandparents' yard.

He jumped from his bike and flung himself down on the front steps to catch his breath.

His grandparents, sitting on the porch waiting for him, knew that something was wrong, but James didn't have the strength to answer their questions.

"What's wrong? What's the matter?" his grandfather asked, and his grandmother kept repeating anxiously, in the tone that worried grandmothers use, "What happened to you? Are you all right?"

When James was able to reply, he blurted out the story of his encounter with the glowing horse.

"Grandpaw, that horse went right through the fence. He didn't jump it—he went through like the barbed wire wasn't even there! And he shone as bright as a harvest moon."

His grandparents listened while James told the whole story. Then they asked him a few questions, and when he had answered, the three of them sat silent for several minutes.

Then his grandfather spoke slowly. "Son," he said, "I

James saw a magnificent white horse that glowed in the dark.

135

know you're upset about what you saw. I would be, too. But I wonder if maybe your imagination was playing tricks on you."

His grandfather continued talking about how powerful imaginations can be, and he talked so calmly and so sensibly that James was almost convinced the glowing horse didn't really exist. Almost.

Their reassuring conversation was interrupted by the sudden appearance of a large, luminous ball.

The ball hovered over the field across the road, moving only slightly. It was very bright. After a few minutes, minutes during which the Austins sat spellbound on the porch, the glowing ball slowly descended and settled in the field. The glow disappeared.

"Let's go see! Get a flashlight. Come on!" Grandfather Austin urged.

The three of them hurried across the road to the spot in the field where they had seen the sphere land. But though they walked back and forth across the field many times, and though they shone the beam from the flashlight all over the ground, they could find no trace of the bright ball.

"Beats me," the grandfather said, shaking his head. "I know we all three saw that thing land in this field, but it isn't here. This wasn't imagination—we all saw it."

As they crossed the road on their way back to the house, Grandfather Austin said to James, "Son, about that horse—maybe it wasn't your imagination. Now I'm inclined to believe you really did see such a creature."

Sleep didn't come easily to any of them that night.

At daylight, James slipped out of the house to make another search of the field before he milked the cows. He could find nothing unusual, not even a blade of grass disturbed.

That very day Grandfather Austin had a severe heart

A large, bright ball appeared and later settled in the field.

attack. He was hospitalized for a long time, and, though he did recover, he had a close call.

The luminous horse and the glowing ball were always associated in James' mind with his grandfather's heart attack. Many people in the community believed the horse and the ball were warnings of some kind, possibly even the warning of approaching death.

After that experience, James and his grandfather became closer than ever. There had always been a strong tie, a deep friendship, between the two, and somehow the unexplained strangeness of what they had seen that night combined with the grandfather's brush with death strengthened their appreciation and their enjoyment of each other.

James shared his plans for entering the ministry with his grandfather—how proud the old man was!—and they talked together about the educational preparation James would need.

His grandfather talked to him, too, about the importance of choosing the right wife.

"It takes a mighty fine woman, a good woman, to be a preacher's wife," his grandfather often said. "Be very careful who you marry."

And, after these talks about marriage, he always added, "Remember that I want to be at your wedding. I want the pleasure and satisfaction of seeing you happily married."

"I'll find the right wife, Grandpaw," James assured him. "And you know I want you at the wedding. It wouldn't be right if you weren't there. But first I must get my education."

So, after he graduated from high school, James went off to Carson-Newman College at Jefferson City to study for the ministry. He was ordained as a minister of the gospel in the Baptist church in 1958.

His grandfather shared in worship services with the young Reverend James Austin, sitting in the congregation and beaming with happiness over the achievements of his grandson.

Although he did experience the joy of seeing his grandson established in the ministry, a series of heart attacks claimed the grandfather's life before James married.

"Grandpaw left me a lot of happy memories," James says gratefully, "a whole lot."

He also left James his pocket watch, a gold Elgin.

James treasured the watch because it had belonged to his beloved Grandpaw, but he didn't use it: gold pocket watches weren't stylish then. He put the watch away in a box, a sort of a jewelry box, in his chest of drawers.

Then, some five or six years later, the girl came along, the right girl, the one James had been waiting for.

Miss Lipscomb and the Rev. Mr. Austin were married at the Cedar Grove Baptist Church at Kingston on January 24, 1965. It was a beautiful wedding, and James was very happy, but he kept wishing his grandfather could have been present.

He kept remembering how Grandpaw used to say, "I want to be present at your wedding. I want to give my blessing to you and your bride."

After their honeymoon in Washington and New York, the couple returned to the rural pastorium near Kingston, the house that James had told his bride "just might be haunted."

They were preparing for bed the first night of their occupancy of the pastorium when they both heard a peculiar noise, a sort of scraping or clicking sound.

James thought some members of his congregation were trying to play a prank on them and were scratching on the window screen.

He ran outside to catch the pranksters, but nobody was there. He circled the house a time or two, stood silent to listen, and went around the house in the opposite direction. He saw and heard nothing.

But when he went back into the bedroom, the sound reoccurred.

Again he searched the premises, and again he found nothing. He was beginning to wonder if he should have teased about the possibility of ghosts.

He reentered the bedroom and, while trying to identify the sound and locate its source, walked over to the chest of drawers. The sound was louder there and more distinct.

"It's somebody winding a watch—Grandpaw's watch!" James exclaimed. It couldn't be—yet—

He snatched open a drawer and took out his jewelry box. He raised the top of the box and lifted out the watch, Grandpaw's gift watch that hadn't been out of the box for five years or more. The watch was tightly wound and it was running.

And it had the correct time: 11:55, it registered.

Somehow Grandpaw seemed very near, as though he had come to give his promised blessing to the young couple.

The white marble mausoleum in Cleveland is marred by red streaks, a reminder of the tragedy that stalked the Craigmiles family.

Stains on the Mausoleum

In downtown Cleveland, just to the rear of Saint Luke's Episcopal Church, is a marble mausoleum which, through the years, has attracted more attention than has the stately church itself.

The mausoleum is the burial place of four members of the Craigmiles family, each of whom died tragically. Its white surface is marred by streaks of red, a red the color of blood. Some residents of Cleveland say the stains appeared after deaths in the family, and the story is that the dark spots are reminders of the sorrow that marked their lives.

Their lives, those of Mr. and Mrs. Craigmiles, started out happily enough with no hint of the heartbreak that was to haunt their later years.

John Henderson Craigmiles was twenty-five years old, a handsome man, when he came to Cleveland from Dalton, Georgia, back in 1850. He and his brother, Pleasant M. Craigmiles, operated a successful mercantile business in Cleveland, and the young man made both money and friends.

141

John, despite his business success, was restless. He was ambitious and adventurous, and he was too young to be ready to settle down in Cleveland. So when news began seeping back to Tennessee of the California gold rush and of the fortunes to be made in that far western state, John Craigmiles could bear the routine sameness of small-town business no longer: he had to be a part of the excitement of the gold rush.

Prospecting for the precious ore had no attraction for John Craigmiles. Prospecting, he knew, demanded strenuous labor and was marked by constant hardship. Furthermore, the rewards were extremely uncertain. He had other plans.

Although he had no experience with shipping, John Craigmiles sensed (he had always possessed a good head for business) that ocean transportation would be a profitable venture. So he purchased a fleet of six ships—brigs, they were called—and began trading between California and Panama.

Craigmiles' two-masted ships with their square rigging brought supplies from Panama to California, goods that the miners and other new settlers needed. On their return voyages, the ships carried disillusioned and embittered gold-seekers who, beaten in California, hoped to find their elusive fortunes in Central America.

It was a lucrative business. Craigmiles sold his imports from Panama at handsome profits in California, and though his California-to-Panama passengers did not always fill his vessels, he did make money on their passages.

Then, at the height of his prosperity, misfortune befell the youthful shipping magnate. Mutinous crews hijacked five of his ships at sea, taking the ships and the cargoes for their own.

Claims by creditors wiped out the fortune Craigmiles had made, but Craigmiles himself was not defeated. He borrowed a stake of $600 from his brother, Green Craigmiles, and set out to recoup his losses.

"I'll make money with the one brig I have left," he promised his brother. And he did.

John Henderson Craigmiles went back to Cleveland in 1857 a very, very wealthy man.

Soon after his return to Cleveland, John began "keeping company," as the expression was, with Miss Adelia Thompson, daughter of Dr. and Mrs. Gideon Blackburn Thompson. They were married on December 18, 1860.

Almost before their honeymoon was over, the War Between the States (call it the Civil War, if you must) had erupted.

Judah P. Benjamin, Secretary of War for the Confederate States of America, recognized John Craigmiles' business acumen and appointed him chief commissary agent. He held that post through the entire four years of the war.

Once again John Craigmiles teamed up with his brother, Green Craigmiles, to take full advantage of his position. According to one account, thought to be quite reliable, Green Craigmiles bought meat at six cents per pound, and John Craigmiles sold it to the Confederate Army for eleven cents a pound. This arrangement is said to have profited them some $20,000 on meat alone in one year.

John Craigmiles increased his fortune in other ways, too. With his brother, Pleasant, as his partner, he speculated in cotton. This venture was highly successful.

It began to be said that John Henderson Craigmiles had the real Midas touch. As did that legendary figure, he liked gold, trusting its enduring qualities more than he trusted the worth of the paper money turned out by the Confederate presses in Richmond. The defeat of the Confederacy, when it came, did not leave him a penniless pauper.

The birth of a daughter, Nina, on August 5, 1864, changed John Craigmiles' life. He had hope for a son, as many men do, but when he saw his baby daughter, he lost his heart to the dark-haired beauty. There were some observers who said he lost his senses, too, that he became completely foolish in his adoration of Nina.

When Nina was baptized on Easter Day, April 12, 1868, at St. Alban's Episcopal Mission, she wore the most elegant clothing that money could buy. Her father was certain that no more beautiful or more angelic child had ever been presented at the altar of any church anywhere.

John Craigmiles was not alone in his devotion to Nina. Her mother, of course, loved the little girl dearly, and her uncles, though they had families of their own, petted and indulged her. In fact, the entire town enjoyed the child and shared her family's pride in her beauty and her accomplishments.

Perhaps no one loved Nina more than did her grandfather, Dr. Thompson. The two often took strolls together in downtown Cleveland (Dr. Thompson liked to show the child off to his friends in the stores and offices), and he delighted in taking Nina with him in his buggy on his calls around Cleveland. The little girl, her dark curls blowing in the wind, sat beside her grandfather on those outings and coaxed him to make the horse trot faster and faster.

"Make him go faster, please, Grandfather! Faster!! Please!" she would beg. Nina had inherited her father's adventuresome daring, and Dr. Thompson, though of a more cautious nature, admired her spirit and usually satisifed her desire for speed by letting the horse trot very fast for several blocks.

Sometimes her grandfather let Nina hold the reins, but usually his strong hands lay on top of her small, gloved

The Craigmiles built one of the most beautiful Episcopal churches in Tennessee in memory of their daughter Nina—Saint Luke's Church in Cleveland.

145

fingers.

They were a grand pair, grandfather and granddaughter, as they rode through the town or toured the countryside. "Look at Nina sitting in that buggy like a little princess," people used to say as the two rode past. It was an apt description.

It was during such a happy outing that tragedy struck.

Dr. Thompson, as he so often did, went by the Craigmiles' house to get Nina to ride with him on his rounds. He got out of the buggy, tied his horse to the hitching post, and went inside the house to escort the child to the buggy.

"Better put her coat on," he told Nina's mother. "The sun is bright, but there's a real touch of fall in the air." It was October 18, 1871, Saint Luke's Day.

Satisfied that Nina would be warm enough, Dr. Thompson took her by the hand and together they walked toward the buggy. Near the end of the sidewalk, he paused to call back to his daughter, "We won't be gone long."

He lifted Nina into the buggy, untied the horse, climbed in beside his granddaughter, and they rode away.

Nina waved goodbye to her mother and threw her a kiss as they rounded the corner. She waved at other friends along their route that sunny afternoon.

Nobody knows exactly how the accident happened. Perhaps Nina and her grandfather, laughing together over a shared secret, forgot they were approaching the railroad tracks. Perhaps the horse shied suddenly. Perhaps Nina had urged the horse to a dangerously fast pace. Nobody knows for sure.

For some reason, the buggy drove straight into the path of a fast-moving train. Dr. Thompson was thrown clear, but Nina was crushed by the cowcatcher.

The whole town grieved.

Funeral services for the child were held at St. Alban's

Episcopal Mission, the same church where she had been baptised three years earlier.

It was an unusual funeral service. After the rector had read the traditional rites for the burial of the dead, had read the familiar Scripture and had led the comforting prayers, a baptism service was held for three adults. John Henderson Craigmiles, Dr. Gideon Blackburn Thompson, and Joseph Green Craigmiles knelt at the altar to receive baptism.

Later, after the acute phase of his grief had eased, John Craigmiles made known his plan to build a church as a memorial to his little daughter. The Episcopal congregation in Cleveland had no permanent meeting place at the time, and it seemed fitting to build an Episcopal church in memory of Nina.

Ground for the church was broken on August 5, 1872, and it was consecrated on October 18, 1874, Saint Luke's Day and the third anniversary of Nina's death.

It is a beautiful church of classic Gothic design. The fine brick and stone exterior, the stained glass windows, the craftsmanship of the interior, the handsome furnishings all reflect the devotion of parents for a little girl whom they had loved and for a God in whom they trusted.

Even before the church was completed, it became a showplace of Cleveland. Natives and visitors alike were awed by its perfection, and, as they admired the structure, they told and retold the story of Nina Craigmiles' tragic death.

John Craigmiles found satisfaction and perhaps a bit of pride in having made possible the creation of so splendid a house of worship, but the satisfaction and the pride did not ease his sorrow.

Almost as soon as the church was completed, Craigmiles began work on a mausoleum in memory of the child. Placed at the rear of the church, the mausoleum is made of fine Carrara marble—two carloads of it—with walls four feet thick.

147

A marble spire topped by a cross rises more than thirty-seven feet above the ground.

Inside are six catacombs or shelves around the walls, and in the center is a sarcophagus modeled by the Italian sculptor Fabia Cotte.

Nina Craigmiles' body rests in the sarcophagus.

Also in the mausoleum are the bodies of Mr. and Mrs. John Craigmiles' infant son, born after Nina's death, who lived only a few hours. The baby was unnamed.

John Henderson Craigmiles' body was placed in that mausoleum after his death in January, 1899. He died as a result of blood poisoning following a fall on an icy street. It was an unusual accident.

His widow (she married Charles H. Cross some time after her first husband's death) died in September, 1928, when she was struck by an automobile on a Cleveland street, and her body, too, was placed in the mausoleum.

People who notice such things say that the first dark stains on the flawless marble appeared soon after Nina's body was placed in the mausoleum.

Those stains, they say, spread and deepened as tragedy claimed other family members: the unnamed infant, John Henderson Craigmiles, and finally Adelia Thompson Craigmiles Cross.

"The stains, like blotches of blood, are like a curse of some kind, a reminder of the tragic deaths of the family," folks say. "And they're sad somehow—and maybe a little frightening—those stains on the mausoleum at Saint Luke's Church."

Seven-year-old Nina Craigmiles went riding with her grandfather and was killed instantly when their buggy was struck by a train.

149

Here are some of the acres on the Bell property in Robertson County, Tennessee, where Kate the witch had her fun.

The Witch Who Tormented The Bell Family

EDITOR'S NOTE: A couple of years ago the ghost Jeffrey, who "lives" in the Kathryn Tucker Windham home in Selma, Alabama, decided to "travel" the South and meet the South's 13 most distinguished (is there a better word?) ghosts. Jeffrey's travels resulted in the popular book entitled Jeffrey Introduces 13 More Southern Ghosts, *authored by Mrs. Windham. Included in that book was an account of the famous witch that long haunted the Bell family of Tennessee. Now, Jeffrey has this thing about introducing the same ghost twice to the same people. So, naturally, even though the witch who tormented the Bell family in Tennessee is one of the world's most famous ghosts, Jeffrey put his or her or its foot down against including the witch in this present book. But—believe it or not—something happened in the printing of this book which the editor cannot explain. The book came out with ten blank pages at the end. So, Jeffrey—sorry, old pal—you are overruled by the witch of the Bell family of Tennessee, and though most certainly you wanted only 13 stories, her story follows.*

It all happened more than one hundred and fifty years ago, but the tales of the Bell Witch are still Tennessee's most famous ghost tales—and its most amazing.

John Bell, victim of the witch's hatred, was an unlikely subject for such a visitation. Born in North Carolina in 1750,

151

he, his wife, and their children moved to Robertson County, Tennessee, in 1804.

Bell bought one thousand acres of land along the Red River, cleared fields, planted orchards, and built a sturdy house for his family. Nearby he built a one-room school where his children (Jesse, John, Drewry, Benjamin, Zadoc, Richard Williams, Joel Egbert, Esther, and Betsy) and his neighbors' children were educated.

John Bell was a very religious man. Neighbors said his life was guided by the Bible and by the American Constitution with the most emphasis, of course, on the Bible. He had family prayers (kneeling) three times daily, and his house served as a gathering place for prayer meetings and other worship services.

On those occasions when he had business in town, he was an imposing figure in his long blue split-bottom coat trimmed with silver buttons, his beaver hat, and his linen stock. His fervent political speeches were credited with helping to win many elections, and he never hesitated to speak out for what he felt was right.

In short, John Bell became wealthy and influential with a reputation for genial hospitality, personal integrity, and Christian discipleship. There was certainly nothing in his background or in his personality to suggest that he would literally be tormented to death by a witch.

Bell first encountered the witch, as the spirit chose to be called, in the late summer of 1817. He was walking through his corn field, estimating the possible size of his crop, when he saw a strange animal sitting between the rows. The creature, which looked like a dog, stared at Bell in a way that made the man feel uneasy. He shot at it, and the animal disappeared among the thick corn stalks.

The episode would probably not have caused Bell any concern had not similar events followed.

Within the next few days one of Mr. Bell's sons, Drewry, saw a huge bird, much larger than a turkey, perched on a fence. A daughter Betsy, on an outing with the other children, reported seeing a little girl dressed in green swinging on the limb of an oak tree near the house. Dean, the trusted Negro servant, told of meeting a peculiar black dog at a certain spot in the road each night.

One summer night in 1818 little Williams Bell, who was only six or seven at the time, was awakened by having invisible hands grab his hair and jerk it with such force that he feared his head was being pulled off. His frightened screams were drowned out by shrieks from Betsy in her room across the hall. She, too, had felt her hair pulled by rough, unseen hands. It was the beginning of months of torment suffered by the lovely young girl who, with her father, became the major object of the witch's wrath.

John Bell, up to this point, had tried to ignore the supernatural happenings at his home. He did not wish to be ridiculed by his neighbors, he did not want to upset his own family by putting undue emphasis on the strange occurrences, he still hoped to find a logical explanation for the events—and each day he half expected the intruder to depart. However, when the unseen spirit terrified his children and seemed determined to do them physical harm, John Bell sought help from his close friend, James Johnson.

"I know you will find it difficult to believe," John Bell told his friend, "but a demon has taken up residence in our house. I need your help in determining what is causing our trouble."

So James Johnson and his wife spent the night with the Bells. Johnson was a pious man, a lay preacher, and he led the family prayers and hymns before they all retired for the night.

No sooner had the household settled down than the

commotion began. That night the spirit demonstrated all her perverse tricks, like a naughty child showing off for visitors. There were knockings, scratchings, gnawings, chairs turned over, chains rattling, covers snatched off, hair pulled, and faces slapped. Nor did the guests escape: the cover was pulled from their bed, and constant bumpings in their room made sleep impossible.

Mr. Johnson became convinced that the deeds were performed by a force which possessed intelligence, and he tried to talk with it. His initial efforts at communication were not successful, but a few months later his theory proved to be correct.

Greatly puzzled by the mystery, Mr. Johnson advised Mr. Bell to make his plight known and to ask other friends to come help with the investigation. From that time until Mr. Bell's death some two years later, the Bell family had a continuous stream of visitors, some neighbors and some from far away. Not one of them was able to rid the house of its hex or to explain the witch's powers.

The visitors, encouraged by Mr. Johnson, tried to entice the witch to talk, to tell what its mission was. After a time it did begin to make a soft whistling sound when spoken to. Then the whistle changed into an indistinct whisper, and finally that whisper grew clear and strong enough to be heard and understood by anyone in the room.

News that the Bell witch could talk created even greater excitement and brought more visitors to the home. Among the visitors none was more famous or more interested in the phenomenon than was General Andrew Jackson, soon to be elected president of the United States.

Jackson was living at his home near Nashville at the time, and when he heard of the cavortings of the witch at the Bell home he determined to go and investigate for himself. He rounded up some of his fun-loving friends to share the trip.

154

They loaded camping equipment and provisions into a wagon (Jackson did not wish to impose on the Bells' hospitality as so many other visitors had done), and the men set out on horseback behind the wagon.

Jackson reined up his horse to call to a friend, "We're off on a witch hunt to John Bell's place. I'll bet you my best fighting cock against a keg of your best whiskey that the witch is a fraud!" And he rode off.

As the caravan neared the Bell home, the wagon suddenly became stuck on the dry, solid ground. No matter how the driver urged the horses or how hard they strained, the wagon would not budge. Its wheels were locked.

Jackson and his friends dismounted and pushed with all their strength, but not an inch did the wagon move. The men removed the wheels to examine them closely, but they found no fault which could account for the stalled wagon.

"It must be the witch," Jackson said, half in jest.

From above the wagon came a caterwauling voice. "All right, General. Go on! I'll talk to you tonight."

The wagon moved easily and quickly toward the Bell home.

Jackson paid his bet—he had found out that the witch was no fraud.

Meanwhile, the witch's conversations increased in frequency and in duration. She enjoyed amazing her listeners with her knowledge of the Bible and of religious matters. She could sing every hymn in the hymnal, could quote any passage in the Bible, and could argue convincingly any question of theology.

She must have been a faithful if unseen attendant at church services, for she would often astound visiting preachers by repeating word for word their prayers, their hymns, their announcements, and their sermons. She was a talented mimic and could copy voices and inflections perfectly.

She particularly liked to mimic James Johnson whom she called "Old Sugar Mouth" because of the "sweet words he says when he prays and preaches."

Perhaps even more amazing than her interest in religion was her custom of reminding guests of events in their past, often happenings that had occurred miles away. In fact, the witch began making nightly reports of all the doings in the community. Many residents, it is said, improved their conduct for fear their misdeeds would be reported publicly by the witch. She seemed to be able to be everywhere, see everything, hear everything and, most dangerous of all, tell everything!

Her religion was only on the surface, however, and did not prevent her from bedeviling Mr. Bell and Betsy unmercifully. She seems to have hated Mr. Bell and to have envied Betsy. The rest of the family she tolerated, and she even had real affection for Mrs. Lucy Bell.

Many examples are recorded of the witch's devotion to Mrs. Bell, but perhaps the most amazing show of concern came during a time when Mrs. Bell was ill with pleurisy. The witch (she was called Kate although nobody ever knew whether the spirit was male or female—the subject of its true identity was one topic the witch refused to discuss) visited Mrs. Bell each morning during her illness and tried to cheer her by singing to her.

One verse from a song sung daily by Kate ended with the words,

> "Troubled like the restless sea,
> Feeble, faint and fearful,
> Plagued with every sore disease,
> How can I be cheerful?"

Neighbors nursing Mrs. Bell never failed to weep at the witch's plaintive, sweet rendition of the sentimental song.

It was during the same illness that Kate, the witch, brought Mrs. Bell a gift of hazelnuts to tempt her appetite.

"Hold out your hands, Lucy, and I will give you a present," the witch's voice instructed.

A shower of hazelnuts fell from the ceiling into Mrs. Bell's outstretched hands. Then, when Mrs. Bell observed that she could not eat the nuts because they were not cracked, their shells were cracked by strong, unseen hands, and then placed carefully on the bed beside Mrs. Bell.

People in the room who witnessed the event looked in vain for openings in the walls or ceiling, but they found no crevice through which the nuts could have come.

A few days later they were equally amazed when a bunch of wild grapes, freshly picked from a swampy thicket, dropped gently on the bed beside Mrs. Bell.

"Eat your grapes, Lucy. They'll make you feel better," the witch instructed.

Mrs. Bell's recovery began almost at once.

But as Mrs. Bell improved, Mr. Bell's health became worse. He complained of a strange affliction. At first he had the sensation of having a stick lodged crossways in his mouth. This was not too upsetting since it occurred infrequently and was of short duration, but as the witch's hatred for him increased, this ailment grew in seriousness.

Mr. Bell's tongue swelled until it filled his whole mouth, making it impossible for him to eat or speak for hours or even days at a time.

In addition, the witch tantalized him in other ways, sometimes snatching off his heavy work shoes, no matter how tightly the laces were tied, and slapping him with such force that his face showed the distinct marks of a handprint and ached for hours.

And all the while Kate boasted that she intended to put John Bell in his grave.

157

Finally Mr. Bell's afflictions, coupled with the constant taunting threats of the witch, sent him to his bed, where he died on December 20, 1820.

His death, witnesses said, was caused by a potent poison which the witch boasted she had poured between his lips during the night. The poison was never identified (even the doctor called to attend the dying man could not classify it), but when a few drops of liquid from the cloudy vial were placed on the tongue of a cat, the creature whirled around, sprang crazily into the air, keeled over, and died.

And the witch's taunting laughter filled the room.

After the death of John Bell, Kate concentrated her devilment on young Betsy Bell.

Betsy, in her late 'teens, was an unusually pretty girl, taller than average and with a graceful carriage. Her eyes were blue and sparkling, and her flaxen hair was long and quite wavy. She was a bright, intelligent girl, always praised by Professor William Powell for her fine school work, and she had a happy, sunny disposition. Or she had until the witch began tormenting her.

Betsy and Joshua Gardner, a handsome young man whom she had known since childhood, were deeply in love. Their plans for marriage displeased old Kate, and she alternately pleaded with Betsy not to marry Josh ("Please, Betsy Bell, don't marry Josh") and threatened her with dreadful consequences if she became his wife ("If you marry Josh Gardner, you will both regret it to the ends of your days").

And so on Easter Sunday, 1821, Betsy returned to a heart-broken Josh Gardner the engagement ring she had accepted from him only the day before. He left the community before the week was out, and the lovers never met again.

After a proper interval, Betsy married her former school

teacher, William Powell, and the two apparently had a good marriage until his death seventeen years later. In 1875 Betsy moved to Panola County, Mississippi, to live with her daughter, and she died there in 1890 at the age of eighty-six.

With the death of John Bell and the termination of the romance between Betsy and Josh, the witch's evil reign in the Bell household ended.

But descendants of John Bell's family still talk about the strange visitation of the witch and of the turbulent distress she caused.

They call it "Our Family Trouble."

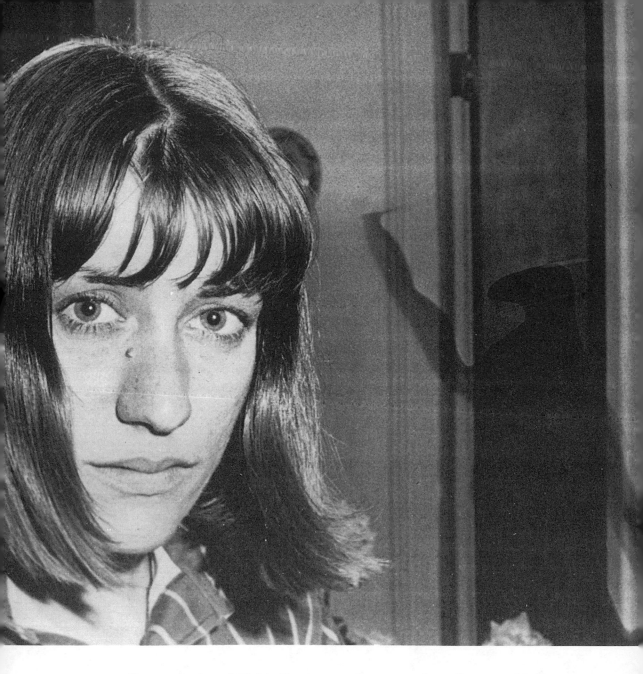

One evening Nikki Davis, a photographer for an Alabama newspaper, was visiting the Selma, Alabama, home of Kathryn Tucker Windham. From a small Mississippi farming community, Nikki (above, left) has always had a reputation for integrity and honesty. She decided to make photographs in Kathryn's house—and two rolls of film were shot that evening. The next day Nikki was developing them casually at her newspaper office when, "Suddenly I almost overturned the developing tank," she explains. One of the negatives she was developing showed a ghost! Nikki learned later that she had discovered Jeffrey (above, right), destined to become the most widely known ghost that has ever "lived" in the South.

Afterword to the Commemorative Edition

In the mid-1960s—maybe because she had publishing friends in north Alabama, or maybe because she thought it would sell and she sure could use the money, or maybe just because she wanted to see if she was up to the challenge—Mother decided she would write a cookbook. *Treasured Alabama Recipes* became an instant big seller, largely because of the stories that accompanied the family collection of recipes.

Shortly after the release of the cookbook, Margaret Gillis Figh, one of Mother's college English professors, called her. "Kathryn, you are going to write another book, and this time it doesn't need to have any recipes in it. It needs to be a book of stories," Dr. Figh told her. "I'll be your collaborator if you like."

About this same time unexplained occurrences began in our house.

I was the only child still at home, my older sister and brother by then off at college. One afternoon Mother and I were in the kitchen rolling out cookie dough. Our house was small but big enough. The narrow kitchen immediately adjoined the small dining room, which opened through paned double doors into the living room.

That afternoon is indelibly imprinted in my memory. I'd floured the rolling pin and Mother had dampened the counter so the edges of the waxed paper wouldn't roll up. We'd sprinkled more flour on the waxed paper—when making cookies nothing should stick to anything else—and the lump of dough was plopped down and ready to roll out.

At that very moment we heard a ruckus in the living room unlike anything I've ever heard since: loud and scratching noises that seemed to come from not one particular area of the room, but rather from a room filled completely with the unsettling sound as though the midget demons of hell might have been turned loose all at once.

We looked at each other, startled, and moved to investigate. Mother wiped flour on her apron as she hurried to open the double doors into the living room. At the first movement of the doors the room became totally silent—no, eerily silent. I was right beside my mother, looking through the panes into the room. "What was that, Mama?" I asked her more out of curiosity than fear. She hesitated. "I have no earthly idea," she said finally.

We stood there for a minute before Mother dismissed it as a squirrel that might have fallen down into the fireplace, though there was no squirrel. There was nothing in that room except the furniture. We went back into the kitchen. As soon as the dough was almost thin enough to make acceptably crisp cookies, it began again, this time louder and with more force than before. And again, the minute Mother pushed the door, it all stopped. Not one item in the room was disturbed. Not one picture was crooked. Not one glass paperweight had fallen from the mantel.

Though Mother and I waited with some anticipation, the remainder of that day was quiet, ordinary. But in the weeks and months that followed, the unaccountable goings-on continued. They began with loud footsteps clumping down the hall, the steps ending abruptly just inside my brother's bedroom with a jarring slam of the door.

Subsequent strangeness took the form of furniture rearranging, not just shifting a bit as it would if a foundation was settling, but honest-to-goodness interior redecorating—beds rearranged to balance dressers moved from one wall to another. Freshly baked cakes flying—not falling, but *sailing*—off the dining room table. We were amazed, entertained, puzzled, but we were never frightened. My brother and sister pooh-poo-hed our stories on their first visits home from college. But as the unusual goings-on manifested themselves to my siblings, they, too, were intrigued.

DILCY WINDHAM HILLEY

My mother was a multifaceted woman.

She taught a Sunday school class and made sure we went to church twice on the Sabbath. She was a believer.

She also was generous, perhaps to a fault. One Christmas we got extra stockings. As always, we drove down later to my grandmother's house in Thomasville, but Mother made an unexpected detour down a dirt road that she chose at random. We saw an African American woman walking with two small children. They were total strangers to us.

Mother stopped the car and asked me to give the children our extra stockings that were filled with candy, toys, and fruit. The children's mother's eyes sparkled.

"Santa Claus has come for you at the store and now he's come here," she told the children.

That was so like Mother. She told me about visiting a poor family with her father, who was a country banker, when she was young. She played in the dirt with the family's children that afternoon, and later she and her father shared in their meager evening meal.

"You're not better than they are," her father told her when they left. "You're just used to better things." She remembered the lesson all her life.

On the other hand, she believed in the supernatural.

I was skeptical of Jeffrey and her stories. Whenever someone asked me if I believed, my stock reply was, "Sure! Jeffrey sent me to college."

163

That always drew a laugh from the visitor and a wry smile from Mother.

One day, I was preparing to leave Selma for a job in New Mexico. My suitcase was packed and on my bed. Knowing that I had a long way to drive and that it would be many months before I saw Mother again, I embraced her in a lengthy good-bye hug.

Suddenly, my suitcase jumped from my bed, flipped over twice in the air, and landed beside me.

Mother and I just stared at each other.

"Jeffrey," she finally whispered. She wore the same wry smile.

I hit the road quickly. After that, I, too, was a believer.

BEN WINDHAM